Dane paused, wondering how to get in. The walls were made of stone and the little windows were shuttered. Then he remembered the woman hadn't been in darkness, sunlight shone on her. The roof. There must be a hole in the roof. He slipped behind the building on cat's feet. About in the middle of the length of the building and opposite the door on the other side, he laid down his submachine gun, bent his knees, and jumped. The roof stood about a foot and a half above his head. His hands caught the edge, and using his powerful shoulder muscles, he pulled his head up. He looked down into the room through the hole. The woman sat below him, her gaze fixed on the door. He located the spot from where the bullet came, and saw an Arab barricaded in the corner. Dane had a clear view of him. Using utmost care, he pulled his pistol out, aimed, and shot. The Arab fell.

Dwayne Straw

Dane Shaw Series

Dilemma in the Desert-revised 2025
Steadfast in Sicily-revised 2025
Intrigue in Italy
Normandy Knockout-coming 2025

Future books:
Freedom for France
Attack in the Ardennes
Bastion in Bavaria
Conflict in Korea
The Fox and the Vixen

Dilemma in the Desert

Dane Shaw War Adventure Book 1

By Dwayne Straw

Dwayne Straw

ISBN 978-0-9911167-4-4

This is a work of fiction and, except for historical personages, any resemblance to persons living or dead are purely coincidental.

Published by Dwayne Straw

Acknowledgements

I wish to thank James, Ann and Catherine for their support and encouragement for writing this book.

Cast of Characters

Corporal Dane Shaw- assistant squad leader
Captain Drew Matthews- Army intelligence
Angelique DuBois- French refugee
Sergeant Andersson- squad leader
Major Lindisl- head of *Gestapo*
Colonel Nuckells- US Army intelligence
Abu Mehouf- Arab guide
Woolson
Fredericks
Tielson
Zabronski
Webster
Captain Heidelstrauss- Lindisl's aide
Ali- Arab leader

Table of Contents

Historical Background

In 1933 Adolph Hitler and his Nazi Party swept into power in Germany. Two of their ideals were: (1) the Germanic race was by nature the Master Race and entitled to rule the world and enslave all other peoples, and (2) Hitler would redress the perceived wrongs done to Germany at the end of the last war. He swallowed up the countries of Austria and Czechoslovakia peacefully, and on September 1, 1939, attacked Poland and thus started World War 2.

By September, 1942, the war had been raging for three years and the Axis, as Germany and Italy with their allies called themselves, were at the height of their power in Europe. They were the masters of most of the mainland and were deep inside Russia, where the Battle of Stalingrad raged. Rommel, the famed Desert Fox, stood at a place called El Alamein, just 60 miles from Alexandria, Egypt, the goal of his African campaign.

By the end of December the situation drastically changed. The Russians surrounded an entire German army at Stalingrad. General Montgomery beat Rommel at El Alamein and the Germans were in full retreat. A combined American and British army landed in northwest Africa and rushed eastward as fast as they could, trying to capture the Tunisian ports before the Germans got there. The Allies lost the race due to an inadequate supply line and the winter rains which turned the terrain into mud as Hitler poured troops into Tunisia, which lies between Algeria and Libya.

The Allied invasion of the French colonies became a diplomatic problem because France, in technical terms, wasn't at war with anyone. Some French units fought hard against the invaders while others gave a half-hearted resistance, recognizing the Americans and British were fighting to restore freedom to their country. After three days the French signed an armistice and fighting ceased.

On January 30, 1943, the Germans attacked French positions at the Faid Pass in Tunisia, North Africa. The French, although they put up a valiant fight, were defeated, as well as several American units who tried to help. Two weeks later, the Germans launched the attack known as The Battle of Kassarine Pass, the first major battle fought by the Americans, who were defeated and routed. Prior to the battle, American intelligence, in some mysterious fashion, learned the Germans were planning a major attack in the south of the country. General Anderson, the British commander and, in

11

the muddled command structure at the time, commander of the bulk of the Allied forces, disbelieved the report and insisted the main attack would come in the north.

Prolog

Two people huddled together in the tiny room, whispering in voices so low if an eavesdropper were present, he couldn't identify the voices, or differentiate if they were male or female.

"You have news?" the older voice queried.

"Yes, they are gathering forces for a major attack," responded the younger voice.

"Do you know when and where?"

"Not yet, but it'll be soon. I'll know more in a few days."

The older one pondered for a moment. "I can send word for an agent to come and pass on the information to him. By the time he gets here, will you have the rest of the information? I don't trust the normal channels any more, especially with something this important."

"Yes, I'll have it by then." The younger one prepared to leave.

"Be careful," the elder hissed. "It's past the curfew."

"Don't worry, I have my pass." So saying, the shadowy figure opened the door and disappeared into the streets of Sfax.

Chapter One

On the evening of January 29th, Angelique DuBois hurried down the street towards the stone hut she'd inhabited for the past month. Curfew time loomed close and the sun lay low in the west. She came from the bazaar, clutching in her arms the meager amount of food she managed to purchase. Experience taught her to wait until late in the day to go food shopping. By then the selection was poor and the best food gone, but the venders were eager to get anything for their produce rather than having it go rotten and throwing it away. Today she purchased enough for two meals, for tonight and tomorrow night. Then she would have to find more. Just a few francs remained in her thin purse and she could only afford to eat one meal a day. Her possessions were as sparse as her coins. She'd bartered away most everything she carried away since fleeing from Gafsa.

Her breath caught in her throat at the remembrance of Gafsa. Looking back, her life seemed idyllic as a schoolteacher there. With enough food and a salary to satisfy her needs, she spent her time instructing students who weren't at all keen on book learning. Then last November the

14

world turned upside down. The English won a great battle far to the east at someplace called El Alamein, pushed the Germans out of Egypt and were now in Libya. Far to the west, the Americans landed in Morocco and Algeria and advanced into Tunisia. Then, as her lip curled in mingled anger and fear, the hated *Boche* swarmed into the country, followed by the *Gestapo*. The school disbanded and her job ended. She hadn't earned any money since mid-November.

She knew for a fact Jews in Gafsa were rounded up and their homes and businesses looted. She witnessed several families loaded into trucks and driven away. Whispers they were no longer among the living were rampant. Rumors abounded the local *Gestapo* commander, Major Lindisl, saw to their liquidation in person. She'd seen Major Lindisl once. His blond hair proclaimed him as one of the so-called superior Master race, his square, blocky build frightening her even at a distance. Because of the fluid battles and hit and run attacks by the French and Americans on the one side and the Germans and Italians on the other, she ran from Gafsa seeking safety, at last arriving here in Faid.

The sound of vehicles interrupted her musings. She looked up to see a line of German vehicles travelling. All day long she'd watched

15

many vehicles and *Boche* move west. *There must be a battle brewing over there.* She shuddered at the thought and wondered if she would need to flee eastward to the city of Sfax to escape the fighting. She hurried even faster towards the abandoned hut she now called home.

All the buildings in the town were the same yellowish sand color as the stony ground, somehow emphasizing the overall gloom of the town gripped in the iron fist of its German masters. The few Arabs in the street hurried to their own homes, and spared her no more than a curious glance. She knew what they saw: a woman over average height, twenty-one years old, with black hair falling down to her shoulders, black eyes and the typical French elegant bone structure. Her normal, willowy figure now thinned down to bones protruding from her skin, showed the effects of her enforced skimpy diet. She didn't think herself beautiful, but her pretty face, combined with her elegance, gave her a charm all her own.

She reached her one room hut and shut the door behind her. She leaned her back against it and took deep breaths, relieved she made it back without trouble. She trembled as she remembered twice before running a gauntlet of staring men.

Then she laid her meager supplies on the

table: a few scraps of smelly goat meat, a handful of overripe dates, a pomegranate past its prime, and a small sack of barley. She tried to use the same merchants for her purchases. She had a sneaking suspicion the proprietress of the barley stand held some back for her, for which Angelique gave profound thanks.

She started her fire and fried the meat, being careful to divide it into two equal portions, and then cooked, with scrupulous care, half the barley. She ate one-half of the meat and the barley she cooked, and split the dates and the pomegranate into equal parts. The whole consisting of the one meal she would eat this day. By then darkness veiled the sky. Since she owned no candles or anything else except the fire to provide light, and no reason to stay up anyway, she stoked the fire to provide some warmth against the cold night and laid down to an exhausted sleep, still hungry.

17

Chapter Two

Captain Drew Matthews of the Army Intelligence Branch sat at his desk in the city of Constantine, reading through a bewildering number of reports of enemy unit movements. *Are they gathering in the north? In the south? Are they even preparing for an attack?* He rubbed his aching temples. The information on his desk remained too fragmentary, too scattered for him to make a judgement. *This is my first assignment here in Tunisia and I can't make heads or tails of it.*

The ringing of his telephone made him jump. He picked up the receiver. "Captain Matthews."

"Captain, meet me in the briefing room," the voice of his superior, Colonel Nuckells, ordered.

"Yes, sir," Drew answered. Before leaving his office, the twenty-six year old checked his appearance in the full length mirror on the door. He stood two inches shy of six feet, thin of build, with light brown hair. A pair of bright, intelligent brown eyes highlighted a good looking face and a square jaw.

He walked down the hall to the meeting room, where he saluted his portly superior. Nuckells returned the salute and motioned to a chair, "Have a seat, Captain." Drew sat down, wondering why he'd been summoned. He didn't have long to wait.

"I have a job for you," Colonel Nuckells intoned in his pompous voice. "We received word an informant gathered important information to pass on to us. We need to send a courier to meet him and bring the information back. I'm choosing you to go because you speak fluent French, I hear." The colonel beamed like he'd given Drew a Christmas present. Surprised by the unexpected order, Drew looked blank as he tried to process the information.

Nuckells continued, "I arranged for an Arab to guide you to your destination. His name is," Nuckells looked down at his report, "Abu Mehouf. He'll lead you to Sfax," again he looked at his report, "to a restaurant called, uh, *Le Belle Francaise*," butchering the name. Drew winced. "The informant, a *Monsieur* Gascoigne, will meet you there. He'll identify himself by the phrase 'The lilies are beautiful by the Loire.' The countersign is 'I prefer the lilies of Garonne.' He'll give you the information and you'll bring it back." The colonel beamed again while Drew still looked blank.

"Sfax is behind the German lines," Drew exclaimed.

"Of course it is. An informant behind our

own lines wouldn't do us much good, would it?" Nuckells laughed at his own joke.

"How am I supposed to get there? How do I get through the German lines? How long do I wait to be contacted? How do I get back?" To Drew these were all important questions which seemed to have been overlooked, the last one being of supreme interest.

Nuckells gave him a stern glance. "You'll check out a vehicle from the motor pool and drive to the front lines. After that, you'll have to use your own initiative. In my years of service I've discovered men with square jaws are more resourceful." He gave an approving look at Drew's feature. A jaw Drew began to wish he didn't possess.

Nuckells went on. "I'm sure you can find out from the front line commander the best places to cross over into enemy territory. Your guide knows the area and can lead you to, uh, Sfax."

"How much does this Abu whatshisname know about the operation?"

"Only he's to take you to the café," the colonel didn't try to pronounce the name this time, "at Sfax and lead you back." He sounded very sure of himself. A few minutes later when Drew met Abu Mehouf and saw his sly face, Drew wasn't at all sure the Arab didn't know much more than he should have. When Drew left the headquarters building after his briefing, he felt better about the operation. He possessed a suitcase of civilian clothes, a large amount of francs in his pocket, and an ID proclaiming him as Etienne Pinochet, a freelance exporter of produce. He felt less sanguine when he got to the motor pool.

"What's this?" Drew demanded of the sergeant, staring at the olive drab painted staff car with white stars on it. "I need a civilian vehicle, not an official Army car."

"Sorry Captain, your requisition is for a staff car." The sergeant didn't sound at all apologetic.

"This is outrageous. I can't fulfill ..." Drew bit his tongue. To continue the sentence would tell everyone within hearing of his going on an undercover mission. "I don't understand why I'm being issued a staff car. Why can't I get a civvie car?" He tried to be reasonable.

"Because we don't have any. All we have are jeeps and staff cars, unless you want a truck?" The sergeant could be reasonable too.

Drew gave the car, the sergeant and the clipboard he held the same fulminating glare before he gave up. He signed the form and grabbed the keys proffered by the too solemn sergeant. Drew slung his bags in the trunk and snapped at Abu in French, "Stick your baggage in here too." Abu tossed in his dirty bag, Drew shut the trunk and both of them moved to the passenger door to open it.

"Here now," Drew remonstrated, "you drive and I ride."

"Drive, *effendi*? I don't know how to drive a car, *effendi*. Camels, horses, and donkeys, yes; vehicles, no." Abu shook his head with a drooped mouth.

Drew stifled a curse and got in under the wheel. Under the open laughter of the men watching, he drove off: an American captain chauffeuring an Arab civilian.

They began the hundred mile trip to Tebessa, the main Allied base in central Tunisia, in the late afternoon. Drew opened the windows to allow air to circulate in the vehicle. The sun shone in the clear blue sky, drying out the muddy ground. He felt thankful for the respite from the cold drenching rain he'd experienced since arriving in North Africa.

As they bounced and jolted over the overused road, in the midst of vehicles rolling both ways all around them, Drew glanced at the barren landscape, dotted here and there with an occasional cactus or thorn bush. Every so often he saw a splotch of green: date trees or other vegetation marking a water source.

Drew glanced at his companion. *Since we're going to be companions for an undetermined amount of time, we should be friendly.* He pointed to a group of shrubs as they passed by. "Those are pretty violet flowers. What are they called?"

Abu shrugged. "Madagascar periwinkle. Why are you going to Sfax?" He turned eager, questioning eyes to Drew.

"We may not have to go so far," Drew temporized. "Why did you hire out as a guide?"

Abu spread out his hands, then grabbed the door when they hit a pothole. "I am a poor man, *effendi,* and need the money. What is so important in Sfax you would risk your life to go there?"

"I haven't been told yet," Drew lied. "How well do you know the area between Tebessa and Sfax?"

Abu held onto the dash as they went over another rough patch of road. "I've travelled between them several times. Your colonel did not tell you why we go?"

"I'm to find out later," Drew replied in a vague tone. Since Abu wanted to talk only about the mission they were on and Drew had no intention of sharing the meager information he knew, conversation languished between them.

When the red sun disappeared behind them and night fell, the thin desert air started shedding the heat and the temperature plummeted. They rolled up the windows and soon after turned on the car heater, grateful for its warmth, or at least Drew was. He looked at Abu, who seemed indifferent to the temperature change. "Didn't you get cold?"

Abu gave an uncomplaining shrug. "Cold, hot, all the same. It is what it is."

Drew wondered if one day he would also become inured to the desert temperature swings.

When they reached the base late in the night, Drew secured supper from the still open mess hall and a place to sleep for the two of them. He lay down, happy at the break in bouncing over the rough road.

Chapter Three

Corporal Dane Shaw of the 26th Regiment, 1st Infantry Division, did not feel at all cheerful. He wandered away from where his company camped and sat down. Picking up a stick, he tapped it on the ground as he reminisced on the last few months. He'd landed at Oran on November 8th in the invasion force and seen for himself the confusion and muddled action which took place. He jabbed the stick in the ground and scowled. *If the French were determined to defend the beaches, the whole invasion could have been thrown back into the sea. It's a good thing the French defenders were of two minds whether to fight us as invaders or welcome us as liberators. Too bad it took a while for them to make up their minds.*

Still frowning, he scanned the countryside around him by the light of the setting sun. The land depressed him. The Tunisian desert lay barren and desolate with little vegetation growing anywhere except near water. The rocky soil, dusty when dry, turned to impassible mud when wet, vehicles sinking up to their axles. To him, an altogether unpleasant place to visit.

By the time the Allies reached Tunisia from

25

the landing beaches in Algeria, the cold winter rains arrived, bogging down the advance. Then substantial German reinforcements arrived, stopping the Allies in their tracks.

Dane jabbed the stick so hard it broke. Now the Americans dangled at the end of an inadequate supply line in central Tunisia. The regiment remained short of everything: spare parts, ammo, clothes, food, and, in his opinion, leadership. The divisional commander, Major General Terry Allen, seemed to be a good general. But the regimental commander, Colonel Andrew Stark, left much to be desired, in Dane's opinion. *His nickname, 'Old', says it all to me. Last night we sat for three hours in trucks, shivering, before being told to get out again and return to our camp.*

The crunch of approaching footsteps broke into Dane's reverie. He looked up to see the thin figure of twenty-one-year-old Private Bob Tielson, a fellow squad member, approach.

"Can I join you?" he asked.

"Sure," Dane replied. He wrapped his arms around his legs and supported his chin upon his uplifted knees.

Tielson sat down. The two men watched the sunset in companionable silence.

"I sure hate it when the sun goes down. It

gets so blamed cold," Tielson complained.

"Yeah, I keep praying for transports to come through so we'll get warm clothing and more supplies."

Tielson felt the earth. "It's surprising how fast the ground dries out. Do you think it's done raining?"

"No. When I visited the battalion HQ yesterday with the captain, there were some French soldiers there. One of them said the rainy season lasts until March. This is just a break. He also told a bunch of us about the happenings around here the last few months. How Admiral Darlan, the supreme French commander in French North Africa, at first refused to join the Allies because," Dane paused for effect, "the British beat the French at the Battle of Trafalgar in 1805 during the Napoleonic Wars."

"What?" Tielson's mouth dropped open as he stared at Dane. "You're joking."

"Nope. He hates the British. Then he changed his mind, came to our side and agreed to fight alongside the Allies. The Frenchman told us about the confusion up north. The French commanders around Tunis, the capital and main port, were bombarded with conflicting orders. Marshal Pétain, the president of France at Vichy, ordered them to aid the Axis and fight the invading

27

Allies. Admiral Darlan ordered them to help the Allies and battle the Axis. Bewildered, they did neither. Then German forces landed at the airports, disarmed the soldiers and took over the defenses."

Tielson looked at Dane with a puzzled frown. "The Germans invaded and occupied France. Why would the French help their enemy?"

"From what I can understand, it's a tricky political situation. Pétain became president of France before their surrender back in '40. So he's the legitimate government of France. But he's also a collaborator and does whatever Hitler tells him. So any French people who want to fight the Germans and free their country could be called traitors."

"Whew," Tielson exhaled. "I didn't know the situation was so complicated."

"Yeah, in contrast in central Tunisia the French General Welvert acted with decision and turned on the German and Italian units there. Though under-equipped and with inadequate arms, he nevertheless put up a spirited defense. He begged General Eisenhower for help. Ike ordered an airborne battalion parachuted in to support Welvert. For several weeks they engaged in hit and run tactics against the superior German forces."

"Then we arrived in Tunisia and here we sit. Because of the lack of reinforcements and supplies we can't advance any further," Tielson said in a bitter tone.

Dane stood up without using his hands and stretched his five foot six inch, one hundred sixty pound frame. "I'm for a last cup of coffee by the campfire before turning in."

Tielson scrambled to his feet. "I don't know how you can get up that way," he grumbled.

Dane grinned. "Just takes practice."

As they walked towards the fire, Dane saw the chubby figure of Private Andy Woolson, another squad member, standing by himself. "Go ahead without me. I'll catch up later," Dane said to Tielson.

Dane walked up and put his hand on Woolson's shoulder. Dane felt the nineteen-year-old shake. "It's okay to be homesick. Everyone here is too," Dane whispered.

Woolson wiped away a tear. "They don't cry about it."

"Believe me, they are on the inside."

Woolson turned a shocked expression to his corporal. "Even you?"

"Yes, me too."

Woolson eyes filled with tears. "I miss my mother most of all," he whispered. "Do you too?"

"It's different for me. I lost my parents

almost five years ago in a car accident."

"Oh, I'm sorry. I didn't know." Woolson hung his head. "I've always been a disappointment to Dad. I've never been what he wanted in a son."

Dane gripped the sufferer's shoulder. "You're doing fine. Keep up the good work."

Woolson gave a lopsided smile. "Thanks, Shaw."

When Dane left Woolson, he saw a group of soldiers talking among themselves. Some of them were his squad members. Dane's cat-like walk brought him to their side before they noticed his arrival. Eugene Fredericks, the brash twenty-year old from Baltimore, boasted of what he would do to the enemy whenever they dared to face him.

"I'll plug so many Krauts they'll have to run a shuttle to replace them," he bragged.

"I'm a one man army," someone else boasted. "Those Germans better start running when they see me coming if they want to live."

Others chimed in with similar claims. Dane read their eyes. Some of what he saw didn't match their comments. Several were scared and trying to hide their fear with brave words.

"Remember to keep your heads down and follow your training," Dane interrupted.

Fredericks jumped at the sound of the voice.

"Where'd you come from? I didn't hear you."

Dane smiled. "You were too busy talking. Be alert and observant. Rely on the other men in your squad. Stay together and you have a lot better chance of surviving and going home." He studied each man in the group. Several expressions showed relief at his comforting words.

He continued to the campfire. When he reached it, he looked around. "Where's the coffee," he asked.

"None here," came the answer. "Try the mess tent."

By now the sun lay below the horizon and the western sky darkened to purple. Dane looked east to where the dark bulk of the Eastern Dorsale Mountains loomed up into the black sky. Stars appeared in the clear air. He felt the temperature dropping and shivered. *At least it doesn't look like rain,* he comforted himself. For the last several weeks, the gray, depressing sky shed its load of water. Sometimes it came down in a drizzle, sometimes in a hard, driving storm, but always cold and chilling to the bone. The rain created the ever-present mud. Mud on the uniforms, mud in the food, great globs of mud sticking to the boots as you squelched through it.

"I need a hot cup of coffee," he muttered

and headed for the mess tent.

He and his sergeant met at the doorway and entered together. They got their drinks and squatted on their haunches.

Sergeant Andersson, a big man with a booming voice, said to Dane, "You mollycoddle them too much, especially Woolson, I saw you talking to him."

"Woolson's coming along," Dane answered in his quiet voice, unconcerned, as he sipped his coffee. He made a face at the warm, not hot, liquid. "He's young and scared and been bullied to the point he thinks he's worthless. But he's gaining confidence. With help he'll be okay."

Surprise splashed across Andersson's face. "How did you learn that?"

"By talking to him, asking questions, being friendly." Dane added, "I do the same to all the men in the squad." He took another drink of the lukewarm liquid. "Any more news?"

"Nah, seems pretty quiet from what the lieutenant said," Andersson replied.

"Maybe too quiet," Dane commented with a faint frown.

Andersson gave a derisive bark of laughter. "The Limeys licked the Krauts at El Alamein, they're done for. Now we're here, the Germans will pull up stakes and skedaddle."

Dane shook his head. "I don't think so. They've been fighting for three years in Poland, France, Russia and Africa. They're tough and experienced. We haven't fought a real battle yet. They're not scared of us. Also, Rommel and his army have arrived in Tunisia. The Desert Fox isn't going to surrender with his tail between his legs or go back to Germany. He's going to hit somebody hard."

Andersson shuddered. Dane noticed and said, "Yeah, it's getting cold again."

"It's not the temperature. I felt like someone walked over my grave." Andersson stared down into his cup. "I haven't told you before. I want to thank you for all the help you've given me. Sometimes I get impatient with preparation work. You've been very capable and taken over much of the responsibility. I appreciate it."

Dane squirmed with embarrassment. "You've taught me a lot about combat tactics. So I guess it makes us even."

Before anymore could be said, a soldier stuck his head in the mess tent. With an excited voice, he announced, "Mail has arrived. Everyone go to your platoons for mail call."

Dane joined the mad rush out of the tent. He

joined the throng around the platoon leader as he read out names and handed out letters. *Will I get a letter from Amy this time?"* he shifted his weight from one foot to the other as he waited with bated breath. At last he heard, "Shaw, Dane." He pushed through the crowd, grabbed the envelope and tore it open. *It's too dark to read here.* He ran to the mess tent where lights glowed. He pulled out the sheets of paper and began reading.

Dearest Brother, Happy twenty-third birthday. I'm mailing this in time for you to get on your birthday, I hope. Isn't it amazing a letter from Iowa can reach England in only a week?

Maybe it took a week to get there, but another three weeks until I got it, Dane grumbled, then resumed reading.

I have the most marvelous news to share with you. I'm expecting!!! The doctor confirmed it last week. Bill and I are so excited! Can't you tell? The baby is due in July. Another family joined the church Sunday and offered us a high chair. People are so kind.

Speaking of food, the new rationing is so confusing. It's all based on points. So many points for this, so many points for that. And they keep changing how many points are needed. It's hard to keep up with.

Bill and I don't care if it's a boy or girl. Just that he or she is healthy and becomes a Christian. I can't imagine the pain of a parent seeing their child on the road to hell, can you?

Dane read through the rest of the pages. Most of it consisted of news about Amy's neighbors, whom he didn't know, or church members, many of which he couldn't recall. She ended with: We pray for you every day. We can't wait for you to meet your niece or nephew. Your loving sister, Amy. And Bill too, of course.

Dane chuckled as he folded the letter. She wrote the same way she talked, jumping from one subject to another, giving headaches to her listeners as they tried to keep up with her.

Dane meandered to his tent amid the sounds of hundreds of men all around him also getting ready for bed. He thought about his effervescent sister, his only relative, with a reminiscent smile before reaching for his Bible. He read the last two chapters of Exodus, about building the tabernacle, and began Leviticus. To his usual prayers this night for the men in his squad, were included a new one for the life just beginning.

Chapter Four

Though they went to sleep late the previous night, Drew and Abu were up early the next morning. When they tried to enter the mess hall an MP, or Military Policeman, stopped them. "No Arabs allowed inside," the soldier wearing a spotless uniform stated with a glare.

Drew drew himself up to his full height. "Private, this man is with me."

"I'm sorry sir, I have orders to keep all Arabs out." The guard didn't sound very sorry.

Drew gave the MP a haughty stare. "I'll have you know Major General Fredendall himself ordered us to work together on an important mission. I don't think you want me to report to him you kept us from eating breakfast."

The unfortunate MP wilted at the mention of the corps commander but rattled on, game to the end. "I would have to have orders from my superior, sir."

"Fine," Drew said in a soothing voice. "You go ask him while we eat." Drew brushed past. Abu followed Drew inside and they got in line. When the server dished up the food into their plates, Drew looked at the skimpy portions. "Is this all we get?"

The mess sergeant leaned towards him. "Food supplies are lean. You want more? Come back for lunch."

"All right," Drew backed down. He and Abu sat down at a table and ate their frugal meal. When they left the mess hall, the MP stared straight ahead, pretending not to see them.

When they reached the car, Drew said, "Abu, stay here while I see what I can find out."

"Yes, *effendi*."

Drew visited several command centers and tried to get some answers from the commanders here at Tebessa, but they seemed to be ignorant of conditions at the front.

"The situation is fluid," they told him. "The main problem is getting through the Eastern Dorsale, the range of mountains between Kassarine and Sfax. There are only a few passes and the French are holding most of them. Your best bet would be to take the Faid Pass."

"Can I draw a civilian vehicle from the motor pool?" Drew asked.

He got a scornful laugh. "Civilian vehicle? Here? They all disappeared years ago. They were either confiscated by the French military or torn down for spare parts."

"Do you have any idea where I could obtain

one?" Drew asked, exasperation rasping his voice.

"Well," the captain Drew conversed with scratched his nose with a thoughtful expression, "off the record, when you get to the Frenchies, you could ask about swapping vehicles with them, sorta temporary like. I don't think too many of their vehicles are marked."

"But, I signed for this car. I have to return it to the pool." Confusion reigned in Drew at this unorthodox suggestion.

"Uh huh, things happen at the front lines, you know, breakdowns and suchlike," the captain said in a vague tone.

"Oh, I see," Drew felt nonplussed at the way things worked at the front. *I'm used to a tidier system.*

He returned to the vehicle and to Abu Mehouf, who sat with his feet on the dash.

Drew scowled at the desecration, but for the sake of harmony held his peace. "It sounds like the Faid Pass is the best route for us, what do you think?" Drew asked to be polite.

"It is what I have learned also, *effendi*," Abu replied.

Drew stared at him in amazement. "How did you hear that?"

Abu waved his arm in the air, "I asked

around, the Arabs know much."

I'll bet, thought Drew as his mouth snapped shut. He stared at the Arab and thought he detected a deliberate vagueness in the answer.

"What do we do when we reach Faid?" Abu asked, eagerness evident on his narrow face.

Drew lowered his eyes. *Abu might have a reason to be so avid about my plans.* "We'll find out when we get there." Drew could be vague also.

They gassed up the vehicle and drove towards Faid Pass, and straight into a battle.

At four o'clock in the morning, the Germans struck the French at Faid Pass. Although the French stopped the main assault, another German force swept through a different pass south of their position and raced towards the French defenders. It was this group Drew ran into.

When he saw dust clouds up ahead, he thought nothing of it. "Must be troops moving up into line," he mused to Abu. They got their first inclination of trouble when they topped a little rise and ran into a column of German tanks.

"Look out," screamed Drew as he yanked the steering wheel. Out of the dust a German tank loomed in front of them. The sound of machine gun bullets screamed as they tore through the U.S. marked vehicle. Drew bailed out at the sign of approaching doom. An explosion roared as the tank fired a round at point blank range. The staff car exploded in a burst of fire and dust. Drew ran, zigzagging through the tank column, hidden by the dust cloud. When he reached cover on the far side of the column, he flung himself to the ground, gasping for breath, shocked he'd made it safe thus far.

Cautious, he raised his head and looked back from where he came. He saw the glow of his burning vehicle through the dust, and he caught a momentary glimpse through a break in the cloud of some German vehicles stopped near it. To his utter amazement the column of German armored vehicles kept moving. He took another look but couldn't see anybody searching for him. *What incredible luck. They must not have seen me running away because of all the dust and the fire.* He risked another glance, trying to see if Abu made it also, but couldn't see anything, *Poor guy; the machine gun must have got him, or maybe the tank shell."* He hadn't liked him, but still felt sorrow at the death of someone he'd known, for however a brief time.

He slithered away, taking advantage of every bit of cover. When he'd covered enough distance to feel safe, he sat down and took stock of his situation. The circumstances were not encouraging. He'd lost his transportation, civilian clothes, and guide. The accidental meeting left him with no food or water and armed with only a .45 caliber pistol. He realized a major attack must be raging and caught him in the middle.

He sat, shoulders slumped in defeat as he thought about an ignominious return to headquarters. How could he explain to Colonel Nuckells he didn't even make it to the Allied front lines? His first clandestine mission ended in failure. He doubted he would ever have another. He felt his pockets to see if he'd missed anything. He pulled out his false ID and the wad of francs. *I still have these, at least.* His head rose as he thought of the possibility of continuing the mission. It would mean traveling the seventy odd miles to Sfax, dodging the enemy all the way, finding civilian clothes, locating the café, making contact with the mysterious *Monsieur* Gascoigne, and returning again. His shoulders straightened and his jaw squared. Nuckells told him to use his own initiative, and he would. The first order of business would be to find food and water, and then start the trek eastward. He took a long look around and began walking.

Chapter Five

All morning long of the 30th, Angelique heard the rumbling sound of artillery fire to the west. She stood at her doorway, listening and watching, but never saw anything until midafternoon when a dust cloud approached the town.

The cloud resolved itself into a caravan of German vehicles with red crosses on them. The lead ambulance stopped in front of her hut and a German hopped out. He looked around and walked up to her door. She backed up into the hut, fear clogging her throat. She stared at him in terror as he entered the hut and looked around He said something to her in German. When she continued to stare at him with uncomprehending eyes, he shook his head and pointed to the door, "*Verlassen, schnell.*" A stretcher party came in, bearing a wounded man. The first man motioned for them to put him on the table. Once placed there, he began examining the patient.

The realization of being evicted from her home so it would be used as a medical station to treat wounded from the battle burst upon her like a bombshell. She staggered as the doctor scowled at

43

her and gestured to the door again. She rushed around the room, gathered her belongings, and dashed outside, almost running into a soldier limping into the hut.

She stood there, looking around with a wild expression, wondering what to do or where to go, while more doctors and wounded arrived. Some soldiers started erecting tents around the hut. Other Germans rousted out the legal owners of other nearby houses and took them over also.

Then she saw a German canteen lying on an open tailgate. She sidled over to it and looked around. Nobody seemed to be paying any attention to her. She picked it up. It felt heavy and gave a reassuring sloshing sound, and then she saw a field ration box. She picked it up too, looked up, and froze.

The first German doctor stood in her doorway, looking at her. For a long minute they stared at each other. Then he looked away and helped another wounded soldier into the hut. She scurried away.

She found a hiding place outside of town and spread out her possessions: one change of clothes, a jacket, a thin wool blanket, a pot, a pan, a plate, a cup, eating utensils, matches, the rest of the food she bought yesterday, the canteen and the field rations she'd purloined. A few personal items completed her meager stock.

She ate a few bites of food, packed everything up into her blanket, sat back on her heels and rocked back and forth. Where should she go? She couldn't remain in Faid. She didn't know anywhere to stay and knew nobody in the town. Should she go back to Gafsa? She'd heard about the Allies and Germans fighting between the two towns. She didn't want to stumble into a battle. How about Sfax? She'd been there a few times in the past two years and it lay miles behind the fighting lines. "Mother Mary," she murmured to herself, "where should I go? Please show me." Then she remembered some acquaintances she'd met at Sfax. Maybe one of them would take her in. Perhaps the Conards, or the Dupleixs, or maybe even the Fauncets would take pity on her. *That's where I should go.*

She picked up her pack, slung it over her shoulder, and walked to the highway going from Faid to Sfax. As she trekked alongside it, a truck sped past her. The German driver called something out to her as he passed. She stopped. "The *Boche* take everything," she said to herself. "They took my country, they took my home, and if I stay on the road they may take me." She shuddered and looked

45

around, trembling with fear. "*Mon Dieu*, if I am near the road tonight, what may happen to me? Think Angelique, think. Let's see, the road curves from Faid to Sfax, so if I cut across, it will save distance. The walking will be harder, but there is less chance of meeting *Boche,* and there should be places where I can find water. That's what I'll do."

So saying, she took her bearings and headed off cross-country. Because of her weakened condition from too many missed meals, she paced herself. She walked about an hour and then rested for ten minutes, repeating the process for the rest of the day.

Nearing sundown, she spotted some green off to the side. She turned towards the promise of water and found a seep with some trees, bushes, and grass growing around it. She dropped her pack, laid down, and rested for a little bit before starting food preparation. With care she built a pile of dry leaves, twigs and branches, breathed a prayer to Mother Mary, and struck one of her precious matches. It flared and died down, and then some leaves caught. With gentle care she breathed on them and some twigs caught fire. When a branch ignited, she added more fuel, being careful not to disturb the tiny blaze.

She felt hungry enough to bolt all the food,

but limited herself to the rest of the food which she purchased in Faid along with a few bites from the rations. With a sigh she closed up the ration box, knowing she must make it last until she reached Sfax. She drank from the seep before dressing for sleep. She put on her other set of clothes over the ones she wore, added her jacket, and wrapped herself in her blanket to protect herself from the cold. Worn out by the happenings of the day, she curled up next to the fire and dropped off to sleep.

Chapter Six

When General Welvert, the French division commander, heard about the attack on his position at Faid Pass, he drove to the town of Sbeitla to beg General McQuillin, commanding Combat Command A of the First Armored Division, for help. McQuillin, nicknamed Old Mac, dithered, saying he needed orders. He called his superior, General Ward of the First Armored Division, who passed the request to General Fredendall, the corps commander, who in turn passed it on to General Anderson, the army commander. Anderson approved the request and sent it back to Fredendall, who almost never left his underground bunker and contented himself with pushing counters around on his maps. He ordered McQuillin to launch an attack, but Fredenhall's orders were confusing, contradictory and sometimes almost undecipherable. They resulted in a fragmentary and piecemeal advance towards the battlefield, which didn't start until noon. McQuillin stopped the advance midafternoon and planned to attack the next morning.

General Welvert begged and fumed, as he heard of his units being destroyed while the

Americans delayed.

***

Dane stood in line waiting for his noon meal when a commotion outside the tent grabbed his attention. An officer appeared in the doorway. "Everyone, to your assembly points, on the double."

Those who were lucky enough to have their food crammed their mouths full as they rushed away. The unfortunate ones grumbled as they ran.

Dane raced to his tent, snatched his rifle and equipment and joined the assembling squad. When he saw Sergeant Andersson approach, Dane asked, "What's going on?"

"There's action at Faid Pass. The French are being attacked."

The lieutenant loped by. "Platoon, into the trucks by squad."

Dane climbed into the truck, sat down, opened a ration pack and began eating.

"Didn't you get a meal at the mess tent?" Andersson asked.

"Nope," Dane shook his head. "Got called away before I got my food."

Andersson's gaze flickered around the vehicle. "Those who haven't eaten yet, grab some rations. I don't know when we'll get time to chow again."

Several of the men followed Dane's example. And then they waited. And waited. After an hour, Andersson, muttering imprecations under his breath, jumped out to ask the platoon leader about the delay.

When he returned, Dane asked, "Didja find out anything?"

Andersson grunted, "Old Stark is waiting for orders from Old Mac."

Dane closed his eyes in frustration. "And what about the French we're supposed to help?"

Andersson shrugged. "Who knows? They're probably being destroyed by the Germans," his tone echoing Dane's feelings.

Ten minutes later Dane heard voices. While he tried to make out the words, the truck started. Then the whole convoy of vehicles moved out.

"At last," Dane said. His elation remained short lived. The convoy lurched towards Faid Pass in fits and starts, with frequent pauses. He ground his teeth in frustration as he stared up into the sky.

Tiny dots high in the air caught his attention. As they became larger he tried to make out the markings to see if they were friend or foe. Yellow flashes from their guns declared them to be enemy planes.

Dane watched with horrified eyes as the

Germans strafed the column. The truck slammed to a stop. "Bail out," Dare yelled. He threw open the rear door and leaped out. Some men followed him while others went over the side of the truck in their hurry.

When Woolson went to jump out, his foot caught and he tumbled to the ground. Dane grabbed Woolson's arm and yanked him to his feet. Together they ran away from the road. Dane glanced behind him. "Hit the dirt," he screamed and threw himself to the ground, dragging Woolson with him.

A nearby truck exploded, sending flames and debris into the air. Smoke funneled into the air from another burning truck. Dane rolled onto his back, staring up into the sky. Several planes performed a pirouette of death above him. Smoke billowed from one airplane. It spun towards the ground. Before it disappeared from sight, Dane caught a glimpse of a white star on its wing. An explosion marked the death of the plane and American pilot.

Two other dots flew away, pursued by five German planes. Six more swooped down for another attack on the motionless line of vehicles. Anti-aircraft weapons were ready by this time. Bullets and shells arched up to meet the attackers.

Pieces of metal falling from a stricken plane glittered in the sunlight. The wounded warrior flew eastward.

The other five pressed their attack. Another truck caught fire and black smoke billowed from it. The last plane in the formation lost part of its tail. Then the rest of the planes followed their comrade to the east.

Dane got to his feet and groaned at the destruction. He went to gather the squad together.

Half an hour later the column resumed its trek. One truck returned to camp loaded with dead and wounded. Survivors from the destroyed vehicles were divvied up into other trucks.

An hour later they were struck again. A flight poured out of the sun. Canon fire tore into unarmored trucks. Again all the vehicles slammed to a stop. Soldiers leaped out and scampered to safety. Machine gun bullets ripped into the swooping aircraft. Two more trucks burned. One plane looped and smashed to the ground amidst cheers from the defenders. The remaining planes disappeared into the distance.

More time siphoned away as the column reorganized. As the lieutenant directed the loading of trucks, Dane heard Andersson say, "Sir, where's our air cover?"

"Forward airfields haven't been built yet." The officer looked away. "There's nothing that can be done at this time."

More waiting ensued. Then they traveled half an hour and stopped again. "Dismount," the company commander ordered as he walked by. "We're bivouacking here."

"What?" Dane jumped out. "Sir, there's hours of daylight left. Why are we stopping?" he blurted out.

"Orders, Corporal," the captain snapped.

"What about the French? They need our help," Dane pleaded.

The officer stood there. Dane read the frustrated anger in his superior's face. "We're to attack first thing in the morning."

Aghast, Dane stared at him. As the captain stalked off, his stiff back telegraphed his feelings about the order.

Chapter Seven

Wary of enemy, Drew lifted his head. The afternoon sun beat down on him. He tried to wet his chapped lips, but no moisture remained in his mouth. After leaving the German armored column, he stumbled upon a German infantry platoon hurrying towards the sound of firing. Lucky for him, the noise of battle directed their attention forward and they missed seeing him dive to the ground behind some rocks. Now he peeked out to see if they were gone. Not seeing anyone, he got to his feet and climbed the slope, taking his bearings from the sun and trying to work his way eastward.

He reached the top and peered over. More German infantry wended their way along the bottom slope, heading northeast. He heard a noise behind him. He turned to see some German halftracks hauling an artillery battery, following the infantry platoon he just avoided. Caught between the two groups, he pretended to be a mole and merge into the ground. He held his breath as the two groups passed by, separated by the ridge with him on top of it.

After they passed, he breathed a sigh of relief about again remaining unnoticed and then slithered down the slope. He took a quick glance around, but none of the Krauts were so thoughtful as to drop a canteen for him. He started walking again, his sweaty shirt sticking to his back.

After about half an hour of trudging, sudden firing ahead and close by startled him. He climbed a vantage point from where he saw a firefight raging no more than a mile away. It looked like the Germans who passed by him were tangling with some French soldiers. He hesitated, wondering if he could sneak close enough to get some water from a dead body. But more Germans appeared and he dismissed the idea.

Forced to go around the fighting, he slipped to his right, but heard in time the noise of an approaching vehicle. Again he imitated his favorite animal and planted himself in the ground. More Germans passed by, hurrying into the fray.

He sat up and wiped his face. "Drew, old boy," he said to himself, "you've had more breaks today than any one has a right to. You'd better mind your p's and q's before you run out of luck."

He made a sudden move to get to his feet when a bullet splatted by his head. Shocked, he spun around to see an Arab mounted on a camel not a hundred yards away, drawing another bead on him. Drew's unexpected move saved him from being killed. He snatched his pistol and snapped a shot a split second before the Arab pulled his trigger. It wasn't because of his skill with a pistol he hit the Arab, spoiling his aim and knocking him sideways in his saddle. The camel took off with the wounded man hanging on. Drew stared after the fleeing sniper. *Why did you shoot at an American uniform? Oh, yeah, at a recent briefing, we were told the Bedouin tribesmen hated the French and were aiding the Germans in hope of becoming independent. I must have been equated with the French.*

Being that as it may, he lost an opportunity to get a water bottle. *It's the best shot I ever made in my life.* He snorted. *Face it, Drew, you were lucky once more. You couldn't do it again in a million years. I'd better hightail it out of here before someone else comes along.*

After another half hour or so, he stopped to take a breather, the rugged terrain and lack of water tiring him out. As he rested, he heard the distant rumble of firing coming from three different directions. He grimaced. *Somebody's taking a pounding, and I don't think it's the Germans.*

Marking where the sounds of battle were coming from, he headed off, trying to pick his way around them. As the sun sank down behind him, two more close encounters with passing Germans forced him to duck and hide. Both times he heard them coming in plenty of time.

With fighting going on all around him, he felt surprised not to find any bodies lying around to rifle for supplies, and he cursed his bad luck under his breath. When night fell the sound of firing died down, his stomach growled and his throat begged for something to drink. He found a place to hole up in some rocks. He spent a miserable night, shivering in the cold and frustrated by his lack of progress, both of finding supplies and making his way to the Faid Pass.

Chapter Eight

Angelique woke in the morning, shivering from the cold. She hurried to perform her morning ablutions, ate a little breakfast, filled her canteen, broke camp and started walking eastward. All day long she staggered up and down the stony hills and crossed dry wadis, dust drying out her throat, perspiration running down her dusty face. When the wind blew, it picked up pieces of grit which stung her face. At each break she took one swallow of water and held it in her mouth, letting the liquid soak into the tissues. When night fell, she made a dry camp, ate her meal and tumbled into an exhausted sleep. Before falling asleep, she remembered the date, January 31. *I wonder what the new month will bring. Will it be any worse than the last three months have been?*

***

The American troops were awakened early in the morning, ate their breakfast, and then waited for orders to attack. Dane busied himself making sure the men were outfitted and ready for battle, his calm demeanor masking his growing unease. He created an excuse to wander around the assembly area. Dismay filled him when he learned the size of

58

the attacking force and he hurried back to his sergeant.

"Sarge," he panted, "only our battalion is attacking here."

"What?" Andersson shocked look mirrored Dane's emotion. "How can a force this small take the pass?"

Fright gripped Dane's heart. "I'm scared we're running into more than we can handle."

Andersson shifted his feet, his expression changing to worry. "Our commander knows what he's doing." The lack of conviction in his tone belied his words.

"Form up," the lieutenant commanded, relaying the order to attack.

"Too little and too late," Dane muttered to himself as he followed Andersson into battle. "Much too late."

The advance kicked off at 0700 hours as the sun rose over the Eastern Dorsale Mountains. Blinded by the sunlight, the attackers bumbled and stumbled forward. At last they seized one ridge. Another loomed in front of them. Artillery pounded the defenders. With a rush the Americans charged this obstacle and carried it. Sheets of fire from a third ridge stopped the attack from going further. German Stukas pounced from the sky bombing the hapless defenders.

All through the morning the Americans clung to the ridge. Too weak to advance in face of overwhelming German firepower and unable to retreat, Dane and the rest of the squad plastered themselves to the ground.

Then a German counterattack smashed into the American line, overpowering the formation and scattering men in all directions.

Dust filled the air and obscured men running around. "Set up the BAR here, cover our retreat," Sergeant Andersson bellowed over the noise of exploding shells and gunfire. The team with the Browning Automatic Rifle plopped down to position the rifle. At the same time, Dane's hoarse voice gathered the rest of the squad into a cohesive group.

Shadowy figures loomed up, shouting German words. They swamped the group around the rifle. Dane heard screaming. For a split second he hesitated. *There's nothing I can do.* He yelled at his squad, "Follow me," and ran away from the overwhelming force.

Shells exploded around them, whether American or German Dane couldn't tell but he figured they were the latter. "Hit the dirt," he bellowed and tried to bury himself into the rocky soil. Explosions shook the ground all around him.

A shell lit a few yards away, showering him with rock fragments. One sharp piece sliced his sleeve, leaving half of his corporal stripes flopping. He ignored the pain from the flying fragments and jumped to his feet. "Fall back," he roared to his squad, then hesitated. *Which way is back?* The sun stood straight overhead, giving him no direction. Dust and smoke obscured the surroundings. The constant shell bursts and noise of unseen vehicles drowned out normal conversation and added to the confusion.

He started in what he thought was the right direction, but halted when two yellowish monsters became visible in the murky air. They were German tanks. He looked at their rear ends as they moved away from him. *We've been overrun,* Dane realized. More shapes appeared around them, some were vehicles and some were men.

"This way," he called to his men as he led the half dozen survivors in a new direction, southeast, he thought. They ran, zigzagging, trading gunfire with half-seen figures, flopping to the ground and gasping for breath, and then rising up and running again.

Figures materialized in the dust ahead of them. Both groups to their shock realized the other to be the enemy. Too close to fire their rifles, Dane with his quick reflexes attacked first, smashing the nearest German's head with his rifle. Then pirouetting with the grace of a ballet dancer, he spun and, with his rifle barrel, speared the midsection of a second German, who doubled up and fell. A third German appeared out of the haze and thrust at him with a bayonet on his rifle. Dane dodged, slapping the weapon aside with his own rifle. He hit the German in the front of the throat with a savage karate blow which crushed the German's larynx. It stopped the German in his tracks and Dane smashed him in the head with the butt of his gun. The German fell, never to rise again. By then the first two Germans were getting up. The one with the bloody head, still on his knees, pulled out his sidearm. The other got to his feet, his face green from the blow to his midsection. Dane leveled his gun and shot them both dead. His gun clicked on an empty chamber.

He heard the sounds of fighting all around him, curses and screams of pain in both English and German. He saw one of his men stabbed, then collapse. Whipping out his own knife, Dane plunged forward. The German slashed at him. Dane ducked under the blade, smashing a fist into the solar plexus with a blow so terrific it lifted the

German off of his feet. With a slash of his knife Dane cut the throat of his antagonist wide open.

He spun and took a quick glance around. All the Germans were down as were three of his own men. A quick check revealed all three were dead. A break in the dust showed more Germans close by. "Run," Dane shouted to his men.

Private Andy Woolson looked down in shock at the crumpled German form at his feet. Surprised by the sudden appearance of the man out of the dust, Andy didn't have time to be scared. His training took over and he reacted without thinking. Now he'd killed a man face to face for the first time ever. Frozen, he stared down at the body when Tielson grabbed his arm and yelled, "Let's go." Andy ran after the others, his mind in turmoil.

At last Dane and the three surviving privates were out of the battle proper. He saw a heap of rocks which promised shelter. "Over there," he directed, and they pounded their way around them. Then they stopped, surprised to see three American inhabitants: two privates and a captain.

Chapter Nine

Drew woke in the predawn darkness, cold, hungry and thirsty. He shivered as he cowered, waiting for the sun to arrive and warm him. Fingering the bills of French money in his pocket, he thought *I'm hungry enough to eat them.* He scanned the surrounding barren countryside. *Not an Arab vender in sight.*

As the sun peeked over the dark mountain mass, an explosion of sound erupted from the north. He gaped as he listened to increasing crescendo of a savage battle. He dithered, *Should I go south and avoid the enemy, or travel north in the hope of finding food and water? Wait a minute.* Drew straightened up. *If there's fighting there, it must be at a pass. I'll bet that's where Faid Pass is.* He made his decision. *I'll head towards the sound. I might run into some Americans who can help me.*

He crept northwards, keeping a careful watch for anyone, moving from one shelter to another. As he traveled, the sun rose higher until it stood overhead. Drew stopped at a heap of rocks. From the racket, he knew he must be near the edge of the fighting. *Still no bodies I can loot,* he lamented. *I don't know which direction is the enemy or friends. Who's attacking who? Who's attacking the pass, Germans or Allies?*

The sound of running interrupted him. He pulled out his pistol as two Americans pounded around the rocky spur. They slammed to a stop when they saw his gun. Drew breathed a sigh of relief and holstered his .45. The newcomers relaxed and slumped to the ground.

Drew needed to clear his throat before he could form words. "Who're you?"

"Private Zabronski, sir," the big man with black bushy eyebrows answered.

"Private Webster, sir," the younger, slender GI replied.

"Captain Matthews," Drew introduced himself. He licked his dry lips, but to no avail. "Do... do you have any water?"

Zabronski indicated his canteen. It sported a hole near the bottom. "No, this took the bullet instead of me."

Webster shook his head. "Mine's empty too."

"How about food?"

The two privates looked at each other.

"I haven't eaten anything since yesterday morning." Drew hated the sound of begging which appeared in his voice.

With evident hesitation, Webster reached into a pocket and pulled out a limp candy bar.

Drew seized it and tore off the wrapper. He took a bite and closed his eyes as he chewed the manna from heaven.

He finished the bar, wadded up the wrapper and stuffed it under a loose rock. Before anymore could be said, more running footsteps were heard. Zabronski swung up his rifle and Drew reached for his pistol when three more Americans appeared. A corporal with flapping stripes and three privates came to an abrupt halt.

The corporal stared at Drew's captain bar. "Sir," he saluted, "I'm sure glad to see an officer." He dropped to the ground, followed by the other three, all of them panting.

Drew returned the salute and croaked, "Corporal." He saw the man's canteen, "Water, please," in his husky voice.

"Uh, yes sir," and handed over his canteen.

Drew started guzzling the water. The corporal yelled, 'Stop," and grabbed the canteen. "Take one swallow and hold it in your mouth," he snapped. "That's all the water and I don't know when we can find more."

Drew looked at him. "It's the first water I've drunk since yesterday morning," he croaked.

The seven of them looked at each other. Drew took another sip. "I'm Captain Matthews, and these are Privates Zabronski, and Webster. They arrived here a few minutes ago."

"I'm Corporal Dane Shaw of the 26th regiment and these are Privates Andy Woolson, Eugene Fredericks and Bob Tielson, what's left of my squad," mixed bitterness and sorrow in his voice.

"What happened?" Drew asked, pointing to the battlefield. While Shaw explained, Drew thought about revising his plans. Trying to make it to Sfax all by himself would run the risk of a single, solitary German soldier destroying the mission. He couldn't keep watch at night while he slept. Anyone coming along could capture or kill him. It would increase his odds of fulfilling the mission if a squad accompanied him. He made up his mind. Shaw finished talking and looked at the captain. "What's your unit, sir?"

"I'm on an intelligence mission," Drew announced, "and I'm ordering you to accompany me. I have to secure vital information and return to headquarters." He looked at their startled faces.

The corporal gulped and said, "Yes sir." His three privates looked at each other with varied expressions, then faced Shaw. It appeared to Drew they would follow their corporal.

"What are your orders, sir?" Shaw asked.

Drew hesitated, at a loss for specifics. "We need to get through these mountains."

"To the other side?" Shaw yelped. "That's the German side."

"Yes," Drew nodded with a firm jaw.

Shaw gulped again.

"Now wait a minute," Zabronski's deep voice interrupted. "I signed up as a soldier, not to be a spy behind enemy lines. I'm not going." He glared at the captain from beneath his shaggy eyebrows.

Drew hesitated, trying to think of a response.

Shaw whirled around. "You signed on to obey orders, and you will obey this one." His voice snapped with authority.

Zabronski stared into Shaw's face. The Russian bear stepped back and his eyes widened. He shut his mouth and subsided into silence.

Drew heard the command in the tone and saw the smaller man's expression. Something fierce and dangerous projected from the corporal and Drew shuddered.

Silence reigned after the confrontation. Drew realized Zabronski was cowed, at least for the moment. *Could I have handled him? I don't know.*

Shaken by his thought, Drew watched Shaw stand up and take a careful look all around. "I don't see anybody in the vicinity." He turned and looked at Drew.

He's waiting for me to say something, but I don't know what.

While Drew fumbled for an answer, Shaw suggested, "Let's pool our resources."

"I lost almost everything." Drew explained about losing all of his gear and how he'd wandered around yesterday and today, avoiding German troops.

After the inventory, Drew felt distressed. There were five rifles with 100 rounds of ammo, three caliber .45 pistols, five canteens (two of them empty), enough food for a day, perhaps two, and some other miscellaneous supplies.

Shaw looked at Webster. "Where's your rifle," he demanded.

"I lost it somewhere," Webster made an excuse.

Shaw's face hardened. "You never, ever drop your rifle. You keep it with you at all times, Private."

Webster sagged away from the rebuke.

Shaw turned towards Drew. "If I may make a suggestion, sir? We're all tired out. We fought a battle today. If we rest now until evening and then spend an hour or two scrounging supplies from out there," pointing to the battlefield, "we would stand a much better chance of making it through the pass in the dead of night."

"Good idea, Corporal," Drew agreed. *Then we'll see what the night holds.*

Chapter Ten

All afternoon long the continuous distant thunder of artillery to the northwest told Drew the battle still raged. *The further away from the pass, the better it is for us.*

The men slept and dozed until dusk, when they broke out rations and ate them cold. When the sun disappeared, Drew saw the corporal looking at him.

After a pregnant pause, he said, "What are your orders, sir?"

"Oh, uh, we should, uh, break up into groups. Look for food and water. I'll take, uh Woolson with me."

Shaw expanded on the brief instructions. "Besides food and water, we need ammo for our guns. Webster, you get a rifle. All of you look for a German greatcoat and helmet; they may help us get through the pass. It's doubtful, but look for a running vehicle. We'l divide up into three groups and meet back here in an hour, sooner if possible. Tielson, Webster and Fredericks, you're one group. Zabronski, you come with me."

The stars were bright in the thin desert air but the waning crescent moon shed little light. As

Drew walked, he found it difficult to make out details of the landscape and pick out suitable targets for their scavenging.

After a few minutes of searching, Woolson exclaimed, "Look over there."

Drew saw the form of a vehicle in the direction Woolson pointed. They advanced up to it and discovered a wrecked German halftrack. It had taken a direct hit, and half a-dozen bodies lay around. Drew searched the vehicle and found six greatcoats and a five gallon can of water.

"We hit the jackpot," he burst out. "Woolson, get their helmets," he ordered.

Woolson hung back. "Do I have to? They're…dead."

"Yes you do. We need them."

Woolson shuddered, but obeyed. He gathered the helmets while avoiding touching the bodies.

Drew continued his search of the vehicle. "Here's some food." He looked again. "Not very much though." Then he spotted some backpacks. "We'd better take these to carry our supplies in."

Loaded up with their finds, the pair trekked back to the rocky outcropping. They dumped their gear and sat down to wait for the others.

"Where are you from?" Drew asked

Woolson.

"Kansas. A farm in western Kansas."

Drew waited, but Woolson didn't elaborate any more. "How did you escape from the battle?"

Woolson's voice became animated. "Corporal Shaw led us out. He told us which way to run. There was so much dust and noise I didn't know which direction to go."

Surprised at the emotion in the other's voice, Drew asked, "You think a lot of him?"

"Yeah, he's the greatest." Woolson's head drooped. "He's the only person besides my mother who gave me encouragement."

Before Drew could ask any more questions, they were interrupted. Webster, Fredericks, and Tielson appeared. As they dropped their loot, Tielson reported, "We found a body of an American. We got his rifle, ammo and some food. We looked around some more but didn't find anything else."

Fredericks broke in. "You were talking about Corporal Shaw when we came up, weren't you."

"Yes," Drew agreed.

"Maybe I should warn you. I think he's got a split personality."

"No he doesn't," Tielson exclaimed and

73

Woolson made a negative noise.

"What makes you say so?" Drew overrode the two.

"Well, most of the time he's quiet and doesn't say much. But when he gets riled, he changes. His eyes, they turn green." Fredericks waved his hands in the air. "I've never seen anything like it before. He emanates this force like, I don't know, like you'd think of a Viking berserker."

Drew looked at the others with incredulous eyes. "Is this true?"

Tielson replied, "When he gives an order, you'd better obey or else. But he's not mean or anything like that. He can be forceful, but he's really good. Sergeant Andersson is great when we're fighting, but doesn't care about details. He left those up to Shaw. Shaw's the one who did most of our training here in Africa and handled all the preparations." Tielson paused, then added, "It'd be wise if you listened to any advice he gives, sir. Like I said, he's really good.

The conversation gave Drew a lot to think about.

Chapter Eleven

"Zabronski, you come with me," Dane ordered when he divided the men. *I need to keep an eye on him.* The other two groups headed north. Dane led Zabronski towards the northwest. After walking for about fifteen minutes, they saw a few lights bobbing in the distance.

"Who do you think they are?" Zabronski asked.

"Judging by the sound of artillery this afternoon, we're behind the German line. They're most likely German medics looking for wounded."

They took a wide detour around the probable danger. Five minutes later, Dane spotted a body. He reached it and squatted down next to the unfortunate casualty. Sergeant stripes on the sleeve marked the American's rank. A submachine gun lay next to the body. Dane picked it up and examined it. *It seems to be in working order.* He searched the body for ammo belonging to the weapon. Some sixth sense made him look up to see Zabronski easing out of sight.

"Zabronski," Dane said in a mild tone, the gun pointed in the big man's direction.

Zabronski stopped. "I thought I saw some

75

bodies over there," he excused himself.

"We'll look there in a minute," Dane answered, then continued pulling ammunition from the body. The cadaver's hand held a canteen. Dane picked it up and shook it. Empty. He touched the ground under the canteen and found it damp. He leaned back on his heels. "Poor guy, they wounded him and he died while taking a drink." Dane sighed and stood up. "Let's find your bodies," he said to Zabronski.

A search in the area produced nothing. Zabronski shrugged, "I must have been mistaken."

"We'll keep on searching," Dane ordered. As they wandered, Dane noticed Zabronski dropping behind. Dane stopped and faced him. "Get up here with me and stop lagging," Dane demanded, Zabronski growled something but obeyed.

After another half an hour of searching they came across a group of dead, mixed American and German. They came away with some food, ammunition, two full canteens, four German hand grenades, two German helmets and one German coat.

Dane checked his watch. "We'd better head back."

A whisper of the sound of running feet sounded their only warning. As both men whirled around, Dane saw three Arabs coming at them. Two of them rushed at Zabronski, while one lunged at Dane with a knife. Burdened with the coat and a helmet, Dane flung them away. He grabbed his foe's knife hand. The Arab's rush caused Dane to fall backwards. He doubled his feet up and kicked his foe in the abdomen. The momentum somersaulted the hapless Arab over Dane's head.

Springing to his feet, Dane spared a glance for his companion. He saw Zabronski smashing in the head of one of his assailants with his rifle. Then Dane's opponent closed on him again.

Dane made another grab for the knife arm but missed, snatching a handful of sleeve instead. He yanked on it as the Arab tried to plunge the blade into Dane, deflecting his aim. The Arab, lithe and strong, wrenched his sleeve out of Dane's grasp.

The battle remained almost soundless, as none of the antagonists wished to draw attention to them by yelling or shooting.

Dane made a grab for his own knife but the Arab lunged at him again. Dane avoided the attack by a surprising agile twist of his body, surprising to the Arab anyway. Dane hooked a right jab to the jaw. The blow stunned the Arab for a vital moment, giving Dane the opportunity to pull his knife out.

They circled each other. Dane made a feint which the other ignored. Again the Arab plunged in. Dane caught the knife blade with his own knife and smashed his left hand into the Arab's face, breaking his nose. The Arab stumbled back and Dane leapt forward, burying his blade into him. The Arab collapsed, dead.

Dane whirled around to see Zabronski, with a fiendish look on his face, grab his foe, wrap a massive arm around his head and snap his neck.

Both Americans took deep breaths. "We'd better get going", Dane said. He picked up the coat and helmet. They made it back to the rendezvous right at the deadline.

"How did it go?" Captain Matthews asked.

"We ran into some scavengers. They must have been looting the dead and wounded, robbing them of their valuables," Dane reported.

"They thought we would be easy targets. They were wrong," Zabronski boasted. "I killed two of them, one with my bare hands." Zabronski flexed his muscles. "Little Corporal here struggled killing his man."

Dane heard the unspoken words from the big Russian. *I'm not afraid of you anymore.*

The captain cleared his throat. "Well, let's divide up the loot and get moving. It'll take us a while to reach the pass." He shivered from the cooling air. "Put the coats on."

Everyone did, grateful for the warmth.

As Andy Woolson fell into line and started walking, he stumbled. Webster gave a tittering laugh and Zabronski sneered, "Learned to walk lately?"

Dane turned and snapped, "Stow the chatter."

Andy hung his head in mortification, his cheeks flushed. For years, his hands and feet seemed too big for him. and he was always tripping over something. His father, big and bluff, ridiculed him for his clumsiness, which only made things worse. When he received his draft notice, his father snorted and said, "Maybe they can make a man out of you."

Young and scared, he made his way to boot camp, which became a nightmare for him. The harder he tried, the more inept he became, and the more the instructors yelled at him. A natural target, the bullies ganged up on him. He cried more than once at night, using his pillow to muffle his sobs.

Then he'd been shipped out of the camp and sent overseas. Of course, he remained seasick the entire passage, which made him the butt of more ridicule. When he arrived in Tunisia, the squad they assigned him to didn't include any of the bullies he trained with, which caused a huge sigh of relief. The big sergeant with the loud voice scared him stiff. He reminded him so much of his father. One day, seeing his struggles, the corporal took Andy aside and in a quiet and gentle voice talked to him. He said Andy was part of a team and they were all relying on him, and he could rely on everyone in the squad.

After that, Corporal Shaw had been quick to offer praise, using his soft voice for any needed correction, never yelling at mistakes Andy made. For once in his life he received encouragement from a male, and life started to improve. His awkwardness declined as he became less self-conscious and more sure of himself. He believed he owed it all to the corporal, and felt hero worship for the kind man with the ready, but somewhat shy, smile.

Andy still had his clumsy moments though, he reflected as he reached up and touched the dent in his helmet. This afternoon, he tripped as he followed Corporal Shaw as they ran from the battle. As Andy fell, a bullet clipped his helmet. If he hadn't fallen he would have been hit and maybe killed. He shivered at the thought and hurried to take his place in line. He didn't want to let his corporal down.

Midnight went past before they reached the western edge of Faid Pass. They watched for a few minutes, but saw no traffic.

"How long is the pass?" Dane whispered.

"The map showed about five miles," Matthews answered.

"Put on the German helmets," Dane ordered. Carrying their own helmets by their side, they walked into the pass. "Sure glad for the dim moonlight," Dane commented.

For a while it went well, the traffic being light and they got plenty of warning to hide among the rocks when a vehicle went past. But then about three-fourths of the way through, they heard a vehicle coming up behind them. The pass narrowed here with no place to hide. Dane hissed, "Keep your heads down and keep walking."

They kept in single file as the headlights of the vehicle illuminated them. They heard it slow down. Dane gripped his submachine gun under his coat, prepared to swing it out and open fire if they were questioned, but once the truck passed them it sped up again. They all stopped and looked at each other, heaving big sighs of relief. They resumed their march and reached the eastern end of the pass without further incident.

81

They saw the buildings of a town ahead of them.

"I'll bet that's the town of Faid," Dane said.

"I'm sure you're right." Captain Matthews stopped. "Let's ditch the German helmets here." They found a crevasse and poked the unwanted items into it. "We'll keep the coats for warmth and to use as blankets at night," he added.

They circled a building with tents around it on all sides. It appeared to be used as a first aid station. They avoided the town and came to the other side where they saw a road leading northeast.

"I remember from the map the road makes a shallow curve before it heads southeast towards Sfax," Matthews said. "If we cut across country it should be safer and shorter." He led the way, not knowing he followed Angelique's path. After traversing a short distance, they stopped and made camp. They ate a few bites then Dane posted guards. "Webster and Fredericks, you keep watch for two hours. Then Tielson and Woolson. Zabronski and I'll take the last watch."

Safe for the time being, they slept until dawn.

Chapter Twelve

A few miles ahead of them, Angelique woke when the sun peeked over the horizon. At first she stared around her, not understanding her surroundings, the mists of a dream of a happier time fading from her mind. Dry sobs broke from her as she tried to reach out to her Mama and Papa, but to no avail.

She squatted on her heels and rocked back and forth with her arms wrapped around her, wailing her dead parents. A German air raid in France killed them and shattered her life. "Why keep struggling?" she asked herself. "Why not lie down and die?" She felt so tired; tired from walking, tired of existing from hand to mouth, tired of life. But she shuddered at the thought of wild animals gnawing on her bones, and straightened up. She wiped her eyes and composed herself, ate some breakfast, took off her outer set of clothes, shouldered her bag and set off again, walking towards the rising sun.

The day turned warm again. She took shorter walks and longer breaks this morning, the previous day's trip taking more of a toll on her weakened strength than she realized. She stumbled up and down slopes, keeping herself oriented by the sun. Once she fell on her hands and knees. She stayed there for several minutes, her head hanging down, sun beating down on her. She listened to the siren call of her weakened body: just lie down, just rest, just sleep. But from somewhere inside of her came the determination she would not let the hated *Boche* defeat her. She needed to get up and keep moving. If she kept walking she would win, and they would lose. She struggled to her feet and started putting one foot in front of the other, her scraped knees adding to her misery.

The sun stood high when she topped a rise and saw below her two buildings. At first her numbed mind couldn't comprehend the vision. Then she saw the front end of a German halftrack sticking out from behind one of the buildings. Terrified, she spun around. The cruel face of an Arab loomed in front of her. She screamed and fainted.

Her faint must have lasted only a few moments, because when she came to she still lay where she'd fallen. Five men surrounded her: three Arabs and two Germans.

One of the Germans spoke in French to the Arabs, "Check and see if there is anyone with her." Two of the Arabs scampered off in obedience to the order, but the one who'd captured her stood his ground.

"She is mine," he stated with his jaw thrust forward.

Before anything more could be said, the other German noticed Angelique's open eyes, said something in German and yanked her to her feet. She stood there swaying while the first German, a sergeant, glared at her and asked in French, "Who is with you?" He shook her to give added force to his question.

"No one, I'm alone," she answered, confused by what she'd stumbled into.

The two Arabs returned and reported, "She is alone, no one is traveling with her."

She tried to shrink away from the Arabs' wolfish looks while the German in charge chewed his lip in worry. "Major Lindisl is not going to like this," he muttered in German to his companion, who shrugged, trying to appear unconcerned.

He replied, "The question is, what happens to her now?"

"We hold her for the major," the sergeant replied, albeit with an uncertain look at his Arab allies. They'd gathered around her, their meaning plain on their cruel faces and lustful eyes. She stifled a scream as she tried to pull away from them, her desperate eyes searching for an escape.

The sergeant stepped forward and ordered in a forceful voice," Leave her alone, the major will want to question her."

The command brought howling protests from the three Arabs. The sergeant stated, "You were hired to be guards, now attend to your duties."

One of the Arabs snapped back, "If we don't get her, we will leave."

The sergeant looked around, trying to search out an answer to his quandary. Major Lindisl would want to know why she came. If he were to find the Arabs gone, perhaps telling other Arabs what lay here, well, the sergeant shuddered to think of the consequences to himself. He hesitated and then shrugged, comforting himself with the fact the major could interrogate her afterwards. "*Ja*, you can keep her tonight, but you will be on guard now in case anyone followed her," he told them in French.

Angelique, horror-stricken at what she heard and overcome by all everything which happened to her, fainted again. After some more discussion, one of the Arabs carried her into the smaller of the two buildings, tied her up and left.

She struggled to consciousness some hours later, at first not knowing her location. Her exhausted body had taken over and she'd slept. Her throat felt parched and she tried to swallow, but to no avail. When she looked around, she saw her canteen hanging on the back of a chair. Her hands were tied in front of her, so she squirmed over and got the canteen. She sat on the floor and held the container between her knees while she unscrewed the top. Being careful not to spill any of the precious liquid, she took sips of water, letting the moisture penetrate the tissues in her mouth and throat.

After satisfying her thirst, she listened with all her might, but all remained quiet. She examined the knot on her wrists. Using her teeth, she loosened and then untied her hands. She made short work of the rope around her ankles and stood, swaying until she regained her equilibrium. Making no noise, she tiptoed to the closed door, cracked it open and peeked out. Nothing in sight. She pulled the door open further. Still all remained quiet with not a sign of anybody.

She slipped out and made her way to the side of the building which couldn't be seen from the larger building. Again she scanned the countryside. Dead silence greeted her ears. She started to scramble up the slope, then heard a surprised yell from her right. Abandoning all efforts at being quiet, she started running as fast as she could. From the corners of her eyes, she saw motion as two Arabs ran to intercept her, one from each side of her.

She didn't stand a chance as they ran her down, her weakened body unable to run fast enough to get away from the desert-hardened warriors. She screamed as they grabbed her and dragged her back down the hill, struggling all the way. She continued to scream as they hustled her into the building she'd fled from and tied her to the chair. Tired of her cries, one of them tied a gag over her mouth. They left her while helpless tears streamed down her face.

Sometime later the opening door startled her. An Arab entered, the door closing behind him. Rigid with fear she stared at him as he examined her ropes, making sure they were tight, all the while making comments about what the night held for her. He grinned at her white, shocked face. His evil countenance and words made her lightheaded, ready to swoon. He walked over to a corner of the room and took down a canteen hanging on the wall. He lifted it to his lips when both of them were startled by gunshots outside.

Chapter Thirteen

The same rising sun which awakened Angelique on this first day of February shone down on the busy American camp. Tielson and Fredericks picked up some dry wood. Soon the smell of coffee permeated the air. Dane heated some stew in a pan. After eating and draining the coffee pot dry, Tielson doused the fire and the group began the trek eastward.

Woolson kept his distance from Zabronski. Having been bullied all his life, he'd learned how to spot them and he recognized Zabronski as one.

All morning long Dane kept an eye peeled for aircraft.

"Whatcha looking for?" Tielson asked.

"Enemy planes," Dane answered. "Because of the proximity of the Axis all weather airfields and the distance from the Allied airbases, which are under-supplied and have dirt fields, the Axis enjoy air superiority here in central Tunisia. We need to be careful."

At midmorning they saw greenery and changed course towards it. "Maybe we can replenish our water," Drew suggested. They discovered a seep.

"Hey, look here," shouted Woolson, pointing to a dead fire. The rest of them stood in a circle around it.

Tielson squatted down and felt the ash. "I think it's a day or two old."

"How do you know?" Drew asked.

"The ashes are cold so it's not from this morning. And they're not blown away so it couldn't be from very long ago."

As the canteens were refilled, Tielson scouted around. "I found some tracks," he exclaimed. While the others gathered him, he measured the marks with his hand. He rocked back on his heels and stared in the direction the tracks led. "It looks like one person camped here. The prints are small, too small for most men. My guess is a child or woman."

Dane scowled. "Why would a child or a woman be out here by themselves?"

Drew gave Tielson a puzzled look. "How can you tell? All I can see are some scuff marks."

Tielson smiled up at him. "I grew up in northern New York state. I've spent a lot of time camping out in the woods. I'm not an expert tracker, but I learned enough to figure this out."

"Move out," Dane said. The others started off and Tielson joined them, leaving the mystery unsolved, for now.

A short time later a pair of planes appeared overhead. "Duck!" Dane yelled. He spotted a bank close. The men raced towards it to shelter behind the lee side. Except Drew who stood looking up at the aircraft. Dane switched direction, grabbed the officer's arm and pulled him into the shelter of the bank.

Drew shook his arm free and glared at him. "Why did you do that? I think they were American planes."

"Captain, even if they are American planes, we're behind the German line and they could shoot at us. They're more apt to be Axis. If they identify us, they will also shoot at us and radio our position."

Drew's face flushed with embarrassment. "Oh," was all he could think of to say. The planes kept flying on their route and disappeared in the distance. The men resumed their march.

At noon they stopped for a quick bite to eat. They didn't find any wood so they ate a cold meal. Zabronski and Webster grumbled at having no coffee.

Tielson came to Drew and Dane with a long face. "We're getting low on food; we've only got enough for about another day." The two men looked at each other, and Drew answered, "Thanks for telling us."

Soon they were on their way again. Being fresher and stronger, they made much better time than Angelique, and without knowing it passed by her dry camp in the middle of the afternoon. The sun sank in the west as Drew, leading the column, came to a rise and saw two buildings. He threw himself to the ground, everyone else following suit.

Dane squirmed up next to Drew and peered out. Below him, he saw the two buildings, and three camels chewing their cuds. Then a door opened, and two Germans walked out. One of them called out. Two voices answered him, one of them too close for comfort.

I wonder why he didn't see us. Dane thought.

Unknown to the Americans, the Arab who should have been watching in the direction they came from had his eye on the building holding Angelique, wondering why his companion went inside.

He and the other Arab rose up and walked over to the Germans.

The German who talked spoke in French, and Drew caught enough to think they were the only two Germans there.

Then Dane saw the front of the halftrack. He pointed it out to the captain, who nodded. They slithered back down and joined the rest of the squad.

"It sounded like there's the two Germans besides the Araba. What do you think?" asked Drew.

Dane considered. "They must have food there, and then there's the vehicle. We could drive close to Sfax, hide it out, and then have transportation back to our lines. It would shave days off of the trip. It's a small group out here in the middle of nowhere; they might not be missed for days."

Drew nodded. "That's what I'm thinking too. The buildings are made of stone, we can't let them hole up in them and turn it into a fire fight. We need to eliminate the men outside and get into those buildings fast. Shaw, you take Woolson and break into the building on the left. I'll take Zabronski and take the building on the right. Tielson, Fredericks and Webster give covering fire and shoot the people outside."

Dane hesitated and looked at Woolson. Andy looked back at him with determination on his face and a hopeful look in his eyes. Dane saw Woolson wanted to try. To refuse might destroy what little confidence the boy had gained in the last few months. Dane nodded his agreement, and in a couple of minutes they put the plan into operation. The four enemies were still outside when the four Americans started slipping closer to the buildings.

Andy gripped his rifle hard and gulped. He watched Dane, silent like a cat, sprint downhill to a boulder. It was only big enough for one person to hide behind. After a careful look, Dane advanced to another boulder. Still the enemy hadn't noticed anything. Dane gestured to Andy, who took a deep breath, rose to his feet, hunched over and moved as quiet as he could to the first boulder. He did it! His heart lodged in his throat. He could do this. He could do something without being clumsy and tripping. With new found confidence he watched as Dane made a rush to some boulders near the target.

Dane peered out, nobody noticed him yet. He caught a glimpse of the captain creeping closer to the other building. He motioned for Woolson to advance again. Andy started a run to join Dane. He tripped and fell.

At once, the Arabs and Germans heard the noise. They turned and stared at the fallen figure for a second. Recognizing the uniform, they raised their guns and gunfire erupted. Dane watched in horror as Woolson started to rise and then fall back down.

Dane saw one of the Germans throw up his hands and collapse. The Arabs ran towards the other building while the captain rushed to head them off.

Dane ran to his building and kicked the door open. He stared into the terrified eyes of a woman, bound and gagged in a chair across the room from him. For a split second he stopped in shock. A movement caught the corner of his eye. He threw himself backwards out the door. A bullet fired from inside missed him, splattering him with fragments from where it smashed into the stone doorway. With frantic haste, he wriggled his way around the corner of the building, away from the firefight raging in front of the building.

Dane paused, wondering how to get in. The walls were made of stone and the little windows were shuttered. Then he remembered the woman hadn't been in darkness, sunlight shone on her. The roof. There must be a hole in the roof. He slipped behind the building on cat's feet. About in the middle of the length of the building and opposite the door on the other side, he laid down his submachine gun, bent his knees, and jumped. The roof stood about a foot and a half above his head. His hands caught the edge, and using his powerful shoulder muscles, he pulled his head up. He looked down into the room through the hole. The woman sat below him, her gaze fixed on the door. He located the spot from where the bullet came, and saw an Arab barricaded in the corner. Dane had a clear view of him. Using utmost care, he pulled his pistol out, aimed, and shot. The Arab fell.

Dane looked to see if there were any others in the room or if the Arab moved. The only movement came from the woman, who stared up at him, wide-eyed. Dane dropped back down to the ground, picked up his submachine gun, and went around the corner. The firing over, he saw the other German down and the Arabs stood with their hands up. He walked into the building and removed her gag. At once she started jabbering in a language he thought sounded French.

"Ma'am, if you don't speak English, we're going to have a communication problem," he said as he cut the ropes binding her.

"*Oui*, I speak English," she quivered, then threw her arms around him and started crying. Startled, Dane stood there for a moment, and then with tender care put his arms around her.

Angelique felt a tender touch for the first time since she couldn't remember when, and sobbed harder.

Dane's heart softened and reached out to this poor woman.

"What's going on?" asked a startled voice from the doorway.

Dane turned his head to see Captain Matthews standing there. "Rescuing a damsel in distress, sir," he quipped.

Drew shook his head in wonder. When she raised her head from Dane's shoulder, Drew caught his breath at her elegant beauty and tearstained face.

Dane looked at her. "What's your name?" he asked in a soft voice.

"Angelique, Angelique DuBois," she answered her rescuer, giving him a wide-eyed look from her dark eyes.

Dane felt his heart thud from the look and her nearness, "I'm Dane Shaw."

She gave a tremulous heartfelt smile. "*Merci, Monsieur.*"

Drew cleared his throat, drawing their attention, "I'm Captain Drew Matthews," and added something in French. At once Angelique started babbling away.

Dane looked in confusion from one to the other. "Sir," he snapped, the victim of a strange emotion, "wouldn't it be better to speak in English so we'll all know what's going on?" forgetting he's the only one not able to understand.

"Of course, Corporal," Drew said with an

uplifted chin, assuaging his own jealousy.

When the three of them emerged from the building, all eyes glued onto Angelique. Fredericks gave a wolf whistle. "Look what the corporal found."

Dane shut him up with a look. He cast a quick glance around. Tielson and Fredericks held guns on the two prisoners. The camels were nowhere to be seen. *They must have been scared off by the gunfire.* He tightened his lips about the missing animals and what it might mean.

He walked over to Woolson and looked down at the body. Bullet holes and sightless eyes proved the teenager dead. Dane grimaced as sorrow gripped his heart. *The poor kid, he tried so hard. Maybe I should've insisted another take his place.* Dane sighed. No, he couldn't have taken Woolson's manhood away like that. The others would have known why he replaced Woolson and the youth wouldn't have been able to hold his head up among them.

Then Zabronski caught Dane's attention. The big man stared at Angelique with hot burning desire in his black eyes. A new and strange emotion made Dane move between them, offering a silent protection to the defenseless young lady. The two men's eyes clashed, then. Zabronski looked away.

Dane became all business.

"Has anyone searched the prisoners?" he asked. By the blank looks he received, he knew the answer. He handed his submachine gun to Drew, approached the first Arab and started searching, Angelique stopped near the two Arabs. Dane saw out of the corner of his eye Fredericks' attention riveted on Angelique. Dane opened his mouth to bark a reprimand when he noticed the second Arab's upraised hand start to move to the back of his neck.

Dane shot him.

His flashing speed as he drew and fired his pistol caught everyone by surprise. For a second, shocked silence reigned. Then Angelique screamed.

Drew started forward, his face becoming red. "What are you doing? We don't shoot unarmed prisoners." he yelled.

Dane pointed to the Arab he started to search. "Tielson, if he twitches, kill him," Dane commanded. He strode over to the fallen body and pulled down the back of the robe. In a sheath hanging between the dead man's shoulder blades a knife hilt showed. "Handy place for a weapon if your hands are up in the air," Dane said in a conversational tone. He examined the harness before removing it, then stood up. Everyone stared

99

at him as he looked around. "Finish searching the prisoner," he ordered. Tielson and Webster complied. They didn't find any weapons, not even another knife hanging down his back.

Dane went and looked at the dead Germans. "I wonder why they were here?" he asked out loud.

Angelique spat on one, her face a mask of hate and fear. "*Gestapo.*"

"*Gestapo?*" Drew queried with a stunned expression. "Are you sure?"

"*Bien sûr*, I am sure."

"Why would *Gestapo* be holed up here?" The three of them looked at each other in perplexity.

"Hey Captain," Fredericks came out of the larger building, "plenty of food in here."

"Good," Drew answered. "Let's check out the halftrack."

Chapter Fourteen

Drew, Dane, and Angelique walked around the building and looked at the halftrack. Seats were fitted in the bed and a canopy to cover them. Drew checked out the cab while Dane and Angelique looked into the bed. There were three cases sitting there. Curious, Dane opened one of them. Silverware, jewelry, wedding rings, gilded picture frames, and other valuables sparkled back at him. Surprised, Dane and Angelique stared at the case. Dane ripped opened up the other two cases. The second contained the same kind of items, but in the third one there were also a number of cloth bags. When Dane opened one of them, money spilled out.

"Well, won'tcha look at that?" said a voice behind them. They whirled around to see Zabronski and Webster looking at the wealth.

Drew hurried from the cab and gaped at the open boxes. "Where did they come from?"

Angelique swayed, her face white. "Oh, those poor people."

The others looked at her. "What do you mean?" asked Dane.

"This must be loot from the Jews. The *Gestapo* rounded them up, and the rumor is they

101

were all killed."

The others were stunned. "You mean they killed all of them, men, women and children?" Incredulous, Drew stared at her.

"Yes," Angelique gave a vehement nod.

"So that's why they're here. Someone's trying to make off with the loot," Dane said in a thoughtful tone.

"Major Lindisl," Angelique breathed and shivered. At their questioning looks she went on, "He is in charge of the *Gestapo* in this part of Tunisia. It is rumored he oversaw the looting and murders." She shivered again. "Oh." Her eyes flew open as she remembered something. "I heard one of the Germans mention Major Lindisl's name." She shivered for the third time.

Dane pulled Drew aside. "Captain, I don't like this. I'd feel better if we left here now."

Drew bit his lip, trying to make a decision. "I don't know, Shaw. Angelique is on her last legs, we have shelter here and it's getting close to twilight. How much further could we go? I think we'd be better off staying here for the night."

Dane looked around, not liking the answer but not seeing a better alternative either. "Yes, sir." Then seeing a pick and shovel, he took them and handed them to Zabronski. "Here, have the Arab start digging graves, and I don't want shallow ones." Dane shut the cases and walked back and into the building, Angelique by his side.

Drew stared after them. He'd noticed everywhere the corporal went, Angelique followed.

"She sure is a good looker, isn't she, Captain?" Zabronski gave a sly grin.

Drew cursed. "Get those graves dug," and stalked off.

Inside the hut, Dane looked around. The main room held a kitchen and table. A door led into a smaller room. He nodded to himself and motioned for Angelique to sit down. She collapsed onto a chair at the table. He gave her a critical look. *The captain's right, she can't go any farther.* Captain Matthews walked in and Dane nodded to him. He turned, saw a coffeepot on the fire and checked the contents. "Would you like some coffee?" he asked Angelique.

"*Oui, Monsieur* Shaw."

"Dane, please," he gave an encouraging smile to her.

"*Oui*, Dane," she gave a trembling smile back.

He poured her a cup and then held the pot up with a raised eyebrow to the captain. Drew nodded and Dane poured him a cup also. He placed the cups on the table and they all sat down.

Drew cleared his throat. "How did you wind up here?"

Angelique shuddered. "I left Faid because the *Boche* took my house. I decided to travel to Sfax to see if I could stay with some acquaintances."

"To Sfax?" Drew sat up straight. "Do you know Sfax?"

She gave him a puzzled glance. "I have been there a few times. Why, *Monsieur* Matthews?"

"Call me Drew." *After all if he can do it, so can I,* Drew thought to himself. Angelique gave him a shy smile. Drew went on, "Have you heard of a café called *Le Belle Francaise*?"

"*Le Belle Francaise*?" she repeated, and then, "Oh, oh yes, I have been there once or twice. Why, mons...Drew?"

Drew leaned forward in his intensity. "I need to go to the café. Could you take me there?"

Angelique drew back in horror. "*Non, non,* how could I lead you Americans into there? We would all be killed." Her nerves were shot and she started shaking.

Dane reached out and took her hand, which she grasped like a lifeline. "Captain, let's wait until she's rested before asking her any more. She's had a bad day. Let her get a good rest tonight and talk to her in the morning."

"Tonight," she repeated, and then her eyes opened wide in terror. "They were, they were going to take turns at me tonight." She howled and threw herself into Dane's arms, hysteric sobs wracking her body. He wrapped tender arms around her and murmured comforting sounds until her crying quieted into hiccups. He raised her head and with tender care wiped her eyes with his handkerchief.

"Is that why they tied you up," Dane asked, gentle concern on his face and in his voice. They were at complete variance with the fury roiling his insides, which he didn't dare show to her.

Angelique shuddered and nodded. "The one you killed, he told me what they were going to do to me. I tried to run away and they tied me up. They gagged me because they were tired of my screaming." She went on to explain how she'd been captured.

Tielson came in, wiping his face. "It sure is hard work digging those holes in the stony soil."

Drew cleared his throat, stood up, and turned to leave the building. As he left, he said, "I'll go take care of the bodies. Shaw, you and Tielson prepare supper."

As Dane and Tielson bustled around preparing supper, Angelique drooped at the table, holding her cup of coffee in both hands. The soldier called Dane held her with such tender care both times she'd flung herself into his arms, and yet she'd felt the latent strength in his arms. They made her feel so safe and secure. She felt her cheeks blush at the thought. It'd been such a long time since she'd felt this way. It also hadn't escaped her notice it was Dane, and not the captain, who issued most of the orders. Dane possessed such an air of command about him; she'd been shocked to discover she stood a little taller than he.

On the other hand, it felt so nice to converse in French with the good looking captain and not have to think up the English words when she felt so tired. She closed her eyes and sagged some more.

With supper prepared, Dane called the others. As they trooped in bringing the prisoner with them, Dane apologized, "Sorry, it's stew again."

Tielson licked his chops. "As long as it's hot, I don't mind."

Fredericks and Zabronski started for the same chair. Zabronski glared at Fredericks, who chose another seat. They started to eat, but no one noticed Dane bowed his head before he picked up his spoon.

When they were done, Dane indicated the

Arab with his thumb. "What do we do with him?" he asked the captain.

Drew looked at Dane with a blank stare. "What do you mean, 'what do we do with him?'"

"Do we take him with us, set him free, or what?"

Drew continued to look blank. "I... I don't know."

Dane looked at Angelique. "Do you know anything about these Arabs?"

"Jackals. They are jackals of the desert," she spat. "They would sell their own mothers for a franc."

Dane looked at the captain. "We can't take him with us, can we?" Drew shook his head. Dane went on, "I know I can't kill an unarmed prisoner."

Drew looked up with a startled expression, "Of course not." he exclaimed. He hesitated, at last saying, "I guess we'll have to let him go. He can't keep up with us on foot."

Dane gave him an enigmatic look, and then asked, "Has anyone seen the camels?"

Drew looked puzzled by the question while Fredericks answered, "I've caught glimpses of them, but they're keeping their distance. I guess they don't like our smell." He laughed at his own joke.

Dane looked back at Drew. "Once we've gone he won't have any trouble catching those camels and following us. I for one don't fancy getting my throat slit in the middle of the night." He gave a surreptitious wink to Drew. "Maybe we can leave him tied up when we depart in the morning for," he paused, trying to think of a place not in the direction they were heading.

"Kairouan," Drew supplied, divining Dane's intention and naming a town to the north. They both noticed with satisfaction the Arab's response while the others look puzzled.

Angelique started to say, "Aren't we…"

Dane halted her with a glance. "We're keeping it a secret for now. Tielson," Dane addressed him, "take the prisoner to the other building and tie him up tight. Angelique, you sleep in the other room. We'll camp out here."

Drew started to get angry at the orders being cast around and opened his mouth, then he shut it. The corporal's commands were logical, and to argue would only make him, Drew, look small. Still, he determined to have a private talk with Shaw about who was in charge.

Angelique caught Dane's arm. "Please, I am so scared," she whispered.

Dane gave her hand a reassuring pat. "I'll

sleep outside your door." She smiled at him, rose, went into the room and closed the door.

Dane started to say something, stopped, and looked at his superior. He'd noticed the officer's expression when Dane issued the last batch of orders. "Shall I set the guard, sir?"

Drew shot him a look from narrowed eyes, but saw no evidence of mockery. "Go ahead, Corporal."

"Zabronski, you take the first watch, Webster the second, Fredericks the third and Tielson the fourth. Two hour watches, and check the prisoner every half hour. Stay outside and remain alert."

When done with the cleaning up and the men were bunking down, Dane pulled a Bible out of his pocket and started reading.

Webster tittered. "Are you going to read us a sermon?"

Dane gave him a level look. "Why, do you want one?" he asked in an even tone.

Webster's laugh died away as he looked at the others and saw no support. Fredericks and Tielson were used to their corporal's habit, and Drew felt surprised to see someone actually reading a GI issued Bible. Dane read for a few minutes, and then went and lay down in front of Angelique's door.

Busy thoughts ran through four people's minds.

Angelique slipped into sleep, dreaming of her hero, the man who rescued her and of his tenderness.

Dane remembered how she felt in his arms and how protective he felt towards her before he, too, drifted off.

Her pretty face and elegance danced before Drew's closed eyes. How he wished he'd chosen the other building and rescued her instead of the corporal.

Lust filled Zabronski. Since first laying eyes on the Frenchwoman, he wanted her. He also thought of all the loot, and how it might wind up in his hands, far away from any retribution.

Georgi Zabronski was the son of Russian emigrants who fled the turmoil in Russia after World War 1 ended. His father beat his wife and children when drunk, and he liked to drink. One night when Georgi was sixteen, his father staggered home. Furious at some imagined offense, he began hitting his son. Georgi, already big and strong for his age, had enough of the abuse. In a fit of rage he beat his father into a bloody pulp. Georgi took all the money in the house and left, never looking back.

He spent the next few years roaming about, stealing things and beating people up. On most occasions, his large size would intimidate his victims. If not, then his crushing blows would win any fistfight. He wasn't all brawn and no brain though. More often than not his cunning stratagems were successful. Although he did suffer from the same failing most crooks have; namely they think they're smarter than honest people. If a woman caught his eye, he wouldn't rest until he took her. Few were the women who escaped him.

Zabronski went outside to stand the first watch. He checked the prisoner and made sure his bonds were tight, and then made his way to the halftrack. He felt his way into the darkness and fumbled with the case which held the money. With a 'creak' the lid lifted. By touch he found a bag and thrust his hand inside, taking a handful of paper notes and shoving them into his pocket.

He stopped. *This is a pittance of what's here. I need a plan to take the whole vehicle and everything in it.* He put the money back, shut the lid and climbed back out. He tried to think of a way to hijack the halftrack. The captain he dismissed as rather weak and inept, the corporal could be handled, but he hesitated. Something in Shaw's eyes gave him pause.

111

Nah, Zabronski shook his head. He could break the smaller man in half like a twig. But to be on the safe side, maybe he should see if he could get some of the other men on his side. Afterwards, well, he'd double-crossed others before. He spent the rest of his watch thinking about Angelique and how to get her into his power.

Chapter Fifteen

Angelique woke up the next morning and stretched. She hadn't slept so well in months. The shocking events of the previous day had worn her out to the point of total exhaustion. With a full stomach and the knowledge her hero protected her all night long, she passed a restful night. *What a wonderful man he is,* she thought to herself with a tender smile, as she pictured Dane's face. So strong, so tender. Then, to her surprise, the face of the captain appeared in her mind, with his rather nice smile. She felt confused. *Why am I thinking of him also? But it's rather nice to have two men's attentions.* She smiled to herself. Hearing the men moving around in the next room, she got up.

She brushed her black hair until it shone and then looked at her two changes of clothes with a moue of disappointment. They were neat, but wrinkled and not very clean. With a sigh, she put on the fresher outfit and made a mental note to wash her things the first chance she got.

When she opened her door, she saw the blanket and backpack in front of her. She looked up and saw Dane. They exchanged smiles. She realized he'd left them there so she knew he kept his word.

113

Her heart swelled at his thoughtfulness. Then she felt other eyes on her, and turned her head to see Zabronski leering at her. His black eyes made her shiver. At once Dane moved between them.

He spoke over his shoulder, "Zabronski, since you're done eating go relieve the captain so he can come and eat."

Zabronski leaned back in his chair. "As soon as I finish my coffee."

Dane whirled around. "I said now. You finish your coffee outside." The two men stared at each other. After a pause, Zabronski got up and stamped off. Dane stared after him with a frown between his eyes. Angelique shivered again and murmured, "You will have trouble with him in the future."

Dane glanced at her. "Yeah, I know."

When Drew came in, the three of them sat down to eat, Angelique between him and Dane, savoring the breakfast. This time she noticed Dane bowed his head before eating. She caught Drew's eye, catching the same surprise she felt. Neither said anything.

"Oh, *Mon Dieu*, you have no idea how good this tastes," she beamed at both of them. "The meals I have been eating the last few weeks," and she rolled her eyes. Drew reached out and touched her hand in sympathy. She turned her hand and gripped his, and then reached out and held Dane's hand. "*Merci*, thank you both, so much," she choked. "When I think of what this morning would be like if you hadn't come." She couldn't go on. The two men, embarrassed at her thanks and also filled with joy at their intervention, couldn't answer either.

Drew cleared his throat (Angelique thought, *He seems to do that a lot.*), "I wondered, you said you knew the café *Le Belle Francaise*. I need a guide to take me there. Could you lead me?"

"How could you go there? You are an American soldier?" she asked, wide-eyed.

"I have, did have, "he corrected himself with a twist of his lips, "civilian clothes and I do still have an ID naming me as one Etienne Pinochet, an exporter of fruit. Would you take me to the café?"

Angelique hesitated, then gave a slow nod. "I... guess I could, but what would you wear?" indicating his clothes.

Drew frowned in concentration. "Do you know of a shop where you could buy me a suit of clothes?"

"*Oui,* but it takes money and I have none."

"I have francs, more than enough."

"Well," she gave a Gallic shrug, "*oui*, I can do that."

115

"Good girl," and he squeezed her hand in relief.

Dane stood up. "In that case, we'd better get moving. With your permission, sir, I'll start loading up." He stepped to the door and ordered, "Tielson and Fredericks, carry all the food to the halftrack. Webster, all the water we can hold. Zabronski, keep watch." Dane smiled at their expressions. "Yes, we're riding the rest of the way."

Before they left, Dane made sure the ropes holding the Arab weren't tight, so he could free himself in a few hours. Then as Angelique and Drew climbed into the cab, Dane said, "Get into the back of the halftrack," to the privates.

Moving as slow as he could, Zabronski stood up, stretched, and wandered to the vehicle. When he at last climbed in, he gave the corporal an insolent look.

Dane stared back at him. "Zabronski," he warned "next time I'll leave you." Dane shut the door and got into the cab.

He drove the halftrack, with Angelique sitting between him and Drew. They traveled cross country, going up and down the ridges. The rough terrain threw Angelique from side to side. Drew put his arm around her to steady her, and she relaxed against him. He saw Dane's frown. Drew couldn't resist giving a superior smile to the corporal. *I'm the one holding her this time.* Then he saw Dane glance at her and his eyes soften. He switched his gaze back to Drew and smiled. Drew realized Dane's concern about Angelique's wellbeing made him glad of Drew's support. Drew's smile twisted as he wondered if he could be so magnanimous if the positions were reversed.

Drew thought of something. "Angelique, I need some practice with my French, could I converse with you?" He gave an apologetic look to Dane, realizing how left out the other man would feel at not understanding the conversation. But he felt he needed the exercise, and he saw in Dane's face he realized it too.

"*Mais bien sûr,*" she replied, and then translated for Dane, "but of course."

Drew hesitated, wondering what to say. She gave him a hint. "Tell me about the United States." He started talking, and as the hours went by he found it easier to speak, and Angelique helped him out whenever he got stuck on a phrase. Her eyes got round as he told about his country. He talked of the vast Texas prairie, of wheat fields in Kansas which extended for mile after mile, of the tree covered and beautiful Smokey Mountains, of the soaring majesty of the Rocky Mountains. He mentioned the Grand

117

Canyon, the Statute of Liberty, and eating oranges plucked from trees in Florida.

"I would like to see your country sometime," she exclaimed.

"Perhaps one day you will," Drew replied.

Angelique gave a shy smile and dropped her head. Then she glanced at Dane.

Meanwhile, in the back of the halftrack, Zabronski kept his mind on the boxes and the girl, trying to come up with ideas on how to possess both. "Whatcha think of the captain?" he asked in the age old grousing voice of the privates discussing the shortcomings of their officers.

Webster tittered, "I don't think he has much of a plan for getting in, much less for getting us out."

"No," Zabronski agreed. "You know, this spying business is supposed to be done by volunteers. We didn't volunteer. If we all get together and refuse to go any further, what could he do?"

Tielson almost bounced out of his seat as the halftrack hit a hole. "We were ordered to help the captain. I'm relying on Shaw, he'll see us through," he said with a confident nod.

"What makes you think so?" Zabronski queried.

"He's GOOD. He's tough and he's smart and he plans ahead. If we get out of this with all our hides, it'll be because of him."

Zabronski subsided. It became apparent when he made his plans, he would have to make allowances for the corporal.

The sun climbed higher in the sky and the day got warmer. The constant shaking and tossing as they went up, down, and sometimes sideways, gave all of them a beating. At last, with the sun high in the sky, Dane asked Drew, "I'm thinking it's time to break for lunch, what do you think, sir?"

"Yes," Drew pointed ahead, "that looks like as good a place as any." Dane pulled into the spot and stopped. The three of them exited the cab and stretched their aching backs. The four privates crawled out from the back of the vehicle with painful bodies.

"Corp," Tielson grimaced , "Did you miss any bumps?"

Dane shook his head in mock sorrow. "I think I did a few miles back. Maybe we should go back and hit it. What do you think?"

Fredericks groaned. "If you do, I'd rather walk the rest of the way." Everyone laughed.

Angelique volunteered, "I can heat the food."

"Thank you," Drew smiled at her.

As she worked, Dane asked Drew, "How much further do you think?"

Drew shook his head. "I'm not sure. According to the compass we've been heading east-south- east. We should either hit the Faid-Sfax Road, or Sfax itself. If we go too far south we'll run into the Mediterranean, but I'm pretty sure we aren't heading that far south. I think by evening we'll be pretty close."

After they ate, they rested for half an hour. Fredericks sat by Angelique, trying to make an impression on her. Her responses to his banter showed she thought him a nice boy, which wasn't the impact he wanted to make.

Eugene Fredericks was a natural born follower. As a youth he'd joined a gang in Baltimore, and he equated leadership with size. The gang leader had been a large kid, and when Fredericks joined the squad he transferred his loyalty to the big sergeant. He always underestimated the corporal because of his small stature. Now, impressed by Zabronski's large frame, Fredericks felt inclined to follow the Russian's leading.

Bob Tielson, on the other hand, did not underestimate Shaw. He recognized early on the ability of the corporal, and realized the better decisions the sergeant made came from the smaller man.

Bob grew up in upstate New York. Since a boy he hunted, fished, and camped in the woods surrounding his home. His parents' main source of income consisted of an orchard of apple trees. A large garden and the game he brought in subsidized their dinner table. His father had gripped his hand hard, and his mother held back tears when they said goodbye to him when he left for the war. He thought of them now, wondering how they were doing. He missed the cool green forest and his home. He also thought of Mary Schubert. They were never an item or anything, but he always liked her, enjoyed talking to her. Several of the other boys in the area were sweet on her, but she never seemed to favor one over another. Maybe he would write a letter to her the next chance he got. Just a newsy letter, to see how she did.

After a bit, Angelique rose to her feet, "*Monsieurs,* I need to take a walk." As she swayed out of sight with her graceful walk, Fredericks gave another wolf whistle.

Twin voices snapped, "Fredericks," and equal glares from the captain and corporal deflated him, for the moment.

When she returned, Drew announced, "Okay everyone, mount up." Amid a series of groans and stiff bodies, the others rose to their feet and hobbled to the halftrack.

Everyone but Zabronski, who continued to lay on the ground.

Dane looked at him, but didn't say a word. When the others were seated, he got in the cab and started it.

Zabronski sat up. Dane put it in gear and started moving. Zabronski jumped to his feet and started running. He dove into the vehicle and Dane gave a self-satisfied smile.

His smile froze as he saw a group of Arabs on camels on a not-to-distant ridge, watching them. The others in the cab saw them too.

Drew shifted in his seat. "This is a German vehicle."

Dane shot him a look. "Yeah, but the uniform wasn't."

"Did they see him?" this from Angelique as she stared at the Arabs with a white face.

"Unless they're all blind, they couldn't help but see," Dane said, anger spiking his voice.

***

As the nine Arabs sat on their camels and watched the halftrack disappear in the distance, the leader squinted his sharp eyes. "That's a German vehicle," one of the Arabs stated in Derja, their native dialect of Arabic.

"But it wasn't a German uniform who jumped into it," the leader replied. "The man wore an American uniform."

"Maybe he's a prisoner?" another opined.

"Son of a donkey," the leader snapped, "since when would a prisoner jump into his captor's vehicle. He would leap out of it." He gave a long look after it. "It appears those are Americans driving a German vehicle behind German lines. I smell profit here, my children. Let's follow them and see what we discover tonight." With an evil grin he led his men after them.

Chapter Sixteen

SS Major Lindisl, on detached duty as head of security in southern Tunisia, rode in his *kubelwagon*, the German equivalent of the American jeep. It topped a rise and he saw the two buildings. "Stop," he barked at his driver. As the vehicle sat and idled, he gave the area a piercing look. He couldn't detect any sign of life nor the halftrack near the buildings. He caught movement from the corner of his eye, turned his head and saw three camels standing on another ridge, snuffing up the wind. He knew something terrible must have happened. The Arabs would never have left their camels behind, even if they departed in the halftrack. "Go," he ordered his driver.

As they stopped in front of the buildings, an Arab came out of the smaller one, shedding a rope as he exited. Fright appeared on his face as he caught sight of the major.

"What happened?" Lindisl demanded, speaking in French.

"Master, they came in shooting, they caught us by surprise, we had no chance," the Arab stuttered.

Lindisl grabbed and shook him like a rag

doll. "Who? Who shot you? Who took the halftrack?"

"Americans, Master," the Arab whined.

At first stunned by the answer, Lindisl recovered right away. He gripped the front of the Arab's robe and lifted him off of his feet. "How do you know they were Americans?" he thundered.

"By their uniforms, Master," the frightened man gasped.

Lindisl threw him to the ground. "Where are the others? Where are the cases which were in the halftrack? Talk, you dog, or you will never speak again."

"Oh Master, the others are all dead," the Arab groveled. He swiveled an eye around the area, "I don't know about the cases. The last time I saw them, they were in the vehicle."

"Why are you not dead?"

"Allah was merciful to me. I fought hard, but they overpowered and captured me. I only now escaped from the bonds. See, the rope is lying over there. Oh, have mercy on me, Great Master. I am your loyal servant."

Lindisl tried to control his mighty anger at having his property stolen. He needed to get to the bottom of this mystery and took a deep breath. "Sergeant," he bellowed at his driver, "go search the buildings, see what you find."

The driver, who'd been trying to make himself invisible, because when the major became angry, he wasn't particular about whom he lashed out at, made himself scarce.

Lindisl regarded the Arab with narrowed eyes. "Why didn't they kill you?"

The Arab shrugged. "I don't know, Master."

"Soft Americans," Lindisl grunted in disgust. *And why were they here?* he thought to himself.

The sergeant appeared. "Nothing, Major." (Dane did a good job of cleaning out all evidence they'd ever been there.) The sergeant disappeared around the buildings.

"Do you know where they were going or what direction they went?" Lindisl asked the frightened Arab.

"No, Master." He brightened, "but I did hear them say Kairouan."

The sergeant returned. "There's been some digging behind this building," he pointed.

Lindisl grunted, "Dog, go dig up what is buried. Sergeant, go with him."

Lindisl went to where he'd parked the halftrack three days ago. With difficulty he followed the faint tracks in the stony soil up to the

126

ridge and looked in the direction they led. "Southeast, not north," he muttered to himself. "That's why they let the dog live. Now why southeast? Are they fugitives from the battle, trying to circle around and make it to their own lines, or are they on a mission? And if on a mission, where to? Sfax lies over there. Or are they heading towards Gabes and the British lines? No, Sfax, they must be heading for Sfax. Why, I wonder?" He turned and tramped back to where the other two were digging. "Who dug this hole?" he demanded.

The Arab looked up with a sweaty face. "They made me help dig, but I don't know what they put in it."

The sergeant looked up. "They buried whatever is here deep, Major." After about ten more minutes the shovel struck something soft. They brushed back some dirt and saw black cloth. In a few more minutes they pulled out an Arab body. After another half hour all five bodies were exhumed. But no sign of buried treasure appeared. Lindisl searched the body of the American but found only empty pockets. He scowled down at it. At last he stood up. "Throw the bodies back in and fill the hole up," he ordered.

As the Arab dropped the last body in the hole, Lindisl drew his pistol and shot him. "He knew too much," he told the startled sergeant. "Throw him in and fill the hole."

As the sergeant covered the bodies, he waited to feel a bullet in his back. But the major stared off into space, anger simmering in him for whoever stole the loot he'd stolen.

Chapter Seventeen

As Zabronski sprawled into the bed of the moving halftrack, he turned the air blue with his cursing.

Webster remarked with a gleam in his eye, "He warned you."

Zabronski scrambled into his seat. "I'll get even with that little," and again spoke several words not used in polite company.

Tielson piped up, "I don't know if you could. He's one tough cookie."

Zabronski glared both of them into silence. After a while he kicked one of the cases. "Makes a fellow think, doesn't it?"

Tielson looked at him. "What do you mean?"

"I mean all this stuff here, just waiting to be picked up."

Tielson shrugged. "It doesn't belong to us."

"You know what she said, the owners were all killed. That means it's finders keepers."

"It means this stuff belongs to the heirs. It's not ours."

Zabronski turned to the others. "What do you think? If all the kids were killed too, then there

129

are no heirs. We have as much right to this as anybody else." Webster didn't say anything, but Zabronski could tell his words had a powerful effect on him; he felt sure he could talk Webster around.

Fredericks gave a nervous shrug. "The corporal would never stand for it, and I doubt the captain will either."

"I'll bet they're planning on keeping it for themselves," Zabronski was quick to plant a seed of doubt in their minds.

Webster gaped at him with wide eyes. "You really think so?"

The other two looked at each other and shook their heads. "Not the corporal," Tielson stated, "and you'd better stop talking about it."

Zabronski shut his mouth. He knew his words would start working on the others' minds, except maybe Tielson's. *I might have to get rid of him. It should be easy to do in the middle of a war.*

***

Up in the cab, Drew once more steadied Angelique. She looked at Dane and asked, "Why do you bow your head before you eat?"

"I'm thanking God for the food," he answered as he dodged a hump.

"Why did you do it for?" she asked again.

"It's God who brought the sunshine and the

rain and caused the grain to sprout and grow. It's God who created the animals which supplied the meat. It's because of his goodness towards us that he meets our needs, so therefore I thank Him and praise Him for it."

Drew cleared his throat. "I don't think I've seen anybody reading their Bible like I saw you read yours. Why do you do it?"

Dane swerved to avoid a nasty bump. *God, please give me wisdom to witness to these two precious souls.* "The Bible is God's Word to us. He tells us how to act towards other people, how to live our lives, and most of all, it explains about Jesus Christ."

"Not everyone can read the Bible," Angelique interjected. "One must have special training to interpret and understand it."

"Why?"

She looked at Dane with a perplexed look. "Because it is too hard to *comprendre.*"

"Is it? Have you ever tried to read it for yourself?"

"*Non*, of course not." She felt shock at the suggestion. Dane pulled his Bible out of his pocket and handed it to her. "Here, you can read this one." Right then they hit a dip and their heads almost hit the roof. They all laughed. "Well, maybe after we

131

stop you can read it."

The afternoon passed as they bounced and jostled their way closer to their destination. Then Drew shouted and pointed to their left. "Look out, there's the highway."

Dane shot a look in that direction and saw the road through a break in the hills, about a mile away, with traffic on it. He twisted the wheel and stopped in a ravine. "That was close," he breathed.

Drew scowled, trying to remember the map. "The road is heading southeast, straight to Sfax. We'll need to stay south of it from here on."

Dane tapped the fuel gauge. "We're also getting low on fuel. I'll get a gas can out and put some in."

"Good idea," Drew agreed. "We all can get out and stretch our legs." They clambered out and walked to the back of the halftrack to let the men out.

Dane jerked to a stop. A expression of horror spread across his face. Startled, the others looked around but saw no danger. "Of all the stupid, stupid, idiotic idiots," Dane shouted, anger so great his whole body shook. "How could I have been so stupid?" Fury transformed his face. He snatched his helmet from off his head and dashed it to the ground. It bounced up and almost hit him.

The others gaped at him. "What's wrong?" Drew demanded.

"Look," Dane pointed to the ground behind the vehicle. Now he'd pointed them out, Drew saw the faint and sporadic tracks of the halftrack in the rocky soil. Tielson gave a soft whistle while Dane raged on. "And I drove straight from the buildings to here. Anybody seeing those tracks will know exactly where we're heading."

"Corporal," Drew thundered, "Get a hold of yourself." The two men glared at each other while Dane took deep breaths. At last calm, he reached down, picked up his helmet and jammed it on his head. "Yes, sir."

"Now, it might not be that bad. The tracks are hard to see and they might be missed," Drew reasoned.

Dane shook his head. "If I can see them a little, it would be a road map to those Arabs."

Drew looked skeptical, but Tielson agreed, "Corporal Shaw is right, sir."

Dane berated himself. "If I'd driven north when we left, it might throw them a little, but I didn't think of it."

"Why are you so worried about leaving tracks from the buildings?" Drew asked.

Dane gritted his teeth. "They must have

been waiting for someone to come and get the halftrack. Whoever it is, will follow us. Plus, there's those Arabs we saw."

"Oh," Drew looked blank for a moment. Then he squared his jaw. "I'm the one in command, not you. It's as much, if not more, my fault as yours. Now, stop blaming yourself and let's come up with a plan."

The two of them moved away from the others. "Sir, if anything should happen to Angelique because of my stupidity..." his voice trailed away as the shorter man turned agonized eyes to his superior. Drew gripped the other man's arm. "We'll have to do our best to see nothing does."

Dane looked up at Drew and regained his composure, "Yes sir, we will."

Drew became amazed at the look of sheer determination on the other's face. He also gave a wry smile at Dane's words. *His first thought is for Angelique. He must be falling in love with her.* Drew squared his jaw. *I'll give the corporal a run for his money.*

Dane took a deep breath and looked around, desperate for a plan. He breathed a silent prayer to God for help. An idea came to him. "I think we'd better ditch the halftrack, sir. If I turn and drive it north and the rest of you head towards Sfax," he pointed southeast, "it should throw anyone off the trail, at least for a while." Now in command of himself, he acted more confident.

Drew considered the suggestion, then nodded his head. "Sounds good to me. We can't be too far away from Sfax now, but I'll go with you. There should be two of us who knows where the halftrack is in case we need it and something happens to you."

They went back and told the others the plan. While the men got back into the vehicle, Drew made sure he helped Angelique into the cab and received her smile as a reward. Dane drove to a place where the rocks wouldn't show footprints. He stopped the halftrack and all the supplies were unloaded.

Drew walked up the ridge and searched all around with binoculars, and then called Tielson up. "See the hill over there with some green showing? There might be water. It's a couple of miles away, head for it and be careful. Shaw and I will meet you there. I thought I saw some movement behind us, but quite a ways off, so watch your back." They rejoined the others and the captain continued, "Tielson, you're in charge. Take the party to the hill I showed you."

Dane added, "And Tielson, if you have any

trouble, I'll back you up in whatever action you take," with a meaningful look at Zabronski.

"I understand," Tielson nodded.

As the two men drove off, Drew recounted to Dane everything he'd told Tielson, "I might have been mistaken about seeing something behind us, though."

Dane shook his head. "I have a hunch you did see those Arabs behind us. I expect them to follow us at a distance and attack our camp tonight. I'm praying this ruse will throw them off the scent, at least for a day or two."

Drew gave Dane a quizzical glance. "Do you pray often?"

"Not as much as I should. Since He is the source of all wisdom and is all-knowing, it makes sense to ask Him for direction and wisdom. James 1:5 says 'If any one lack wisdom, let him ask of God', and I know I need wisdom."

Drew digested the fact of someone liking to pray.

They approached the road with infinite caution. Seeing a break in the traffic, Dane sped across, leaving telltale tracks in the ground.

After traveling about five miles, Dane pulled to a stop. "You know," he said, "I would hate for anyone to stumble over this halftrack and find all this loot. How about if we hide it separate from the vehicle, like in one of those crevasses over there?"

Drew looked at the side of the hill which possessed several such hiding places. "Hey, it sounds good to me. Did God tell you the idea?" he added with a little sarcasm.

Dane shrugged. "I don't know. It came to me when I saw the hill."

Drew stared at him. He knew no such idea popped into his head when he saw the hill, and he doubted it ever would have. *Maybe there is something to this praying after all.* The stony ground didn't show their footprints as they carried the three cases and hid them. It took them only a few minutes, and they were on their way again.

The draw they were in turned northeast at the place where they hid the cases, and they followed it. A few minutes later, they came to the road which went between Sfax and the Kairouan-Sousse road. They reconnoitered and found a draw on the other side. When there was no traffic in sight, Dane drove across the road and into the gully. After about a quarter of a mile, they found a ravine wide enough to drive the halftrack into. They looked at each other and nodded. Dane backed the vehicle in as far as it would go and checked to see if the front end protruded out. It didn't. Dane cut a couple of dead bushes and planted them to hide the vehicle, and then cut two more and the two of them brushed out the tracks all the way to the road. By then the sun lay low in the west, and they started walking towards the rendezvous with the others.

***

Meanwhile, Tielson led the party towards the hill. As they walked Zabronski placed himself beside Angelique. All of them wore a backpack; the men carried supplies and Angelique her clothes and personal items.

"I can carry your pack for you," Zabronski offered.

"*Non*, thank you *monsieur*," Angelique replied as she looked away from his intense black eyes.

"I'm strong, it would be nothing for me to carry it," he boasted. He doubled up his arm, expanding his bicep. "I bet you haven't seen anybody as strong as I am. Two days ago I snapped an Arab's neck with my bare hands." He looked her up and down, his black eyes glittering. "I could as easy carry you, and then you wouldn't be so tired out."

Angelique shuddered, both at the reference to the dead Arab and the suggestion. She did not want him touching her. "*Non*, I can walk." She sped up to catch up with Tielson, but Zabronski kept pace with ease.

"You shouldn't be so standoffish," Zabronski remonstrated. "We're all in this together. We'll all need to work together if we're going to survive this mission. You may be glad I'm so strong and can take care of you," he added with a leer.

"Zabronski," Tielson snapped at the bigger man. "Leave her alone."

"Says who?" Zabronski sneered.

"I do." Tielson glared at him with glacial blue eyes. "The captain put me in charge, and the corporal gave me full authority."

Zabronski hesitated and looked at the others. Judging by the looks he got, it would be him against three. It wasn't time yet. He also didn't care for the 'full authority' phrase. He gave the pair an ingratiating smile and backed off. "I'm just trying to be friendly," he excused himself and fell back into line.

Angelique gave Tielson a grateful glance. She only felt secure in the presence of either Dane or Drew. Comforting warmth filled her from the knowledge that even now Dane was doing his best to protect her. She believed she knew what Tielson meant and hugged herself, her eyes sparkling. But she would make very sure not to be alone with the big Russian.

When they got to the hill, Tielson left them at the foot while he scouted around, but found no sign of life. On the west side of the hill there existed an open, level place, large enough for them to camp in, backed by a sheer face. On the east side of the hill, a stream of water came out and tumbled down into a pool, the outflow running on down the hill. On the same side were some trees, bushes and grass. Tielson knelt and plunged his hand into the water. How warm the water felt surprised him. He took a mouthful of water and spat it out, "Well, it's wet," he said as he tasted the mineral rich liquid. From the top of the hill, he saw the buildings of Sfax in the distance, and estimated they were about two miles away. He went back to the others and told them what he'd discovered. "We'll camp on the west face," he announced, "and wait for the captain and corporal."

"Did you say 'warm' water?" asked Fredericks. Tielson nodded. "Like as in bath water?" Tielson smiled and nodded again. "Good, I haven't had a bath for days, and with a beautiful girl around I need to make the best impression I can."

Tielson laughed. 'Okay, we all can use a good cleaning up. Fredericks, you and Webster go first. Ma'am," he suggested with embarrassment staining his cheeks, "you should remain here until we're done."

"*Oui,*" she answered, sagging with fatigue. "I'll start supper after I rest, if it is acceptable to you, *monsieur?*"

"Yes, yes of course," and he made a hasty retreat.

After Webster and Fredericks bathed, Tielson and Zabronski took their turn, and then the four men cleaned their uniforms. While they were doing so, Angelique took the opportunity to wash one set of clothes and left them hanging on some bushes to dry. By then it was full dark and they started eating. In a few minutes they heard a whistle, and Drew and Dane joined them.

Chapter Eighteen

Major Lindisl reached Sfax late in the night, went straight to his headquarters, called up the *Luftwaffe* (German air force) headquarters, and talked to the on-duty officer. "Have there been any sightings of American soldiers on this side of the Eastern Dorsale Mountains?" he asked.

"*Nein, Herr* Major," the officer responded.

Lindisl hung up the phone and called for his own on-duty officer. "Any reports from the Arabs about an American patrol in this area?" He received the same response. He dismissed the officer with a wave of his hand and sat drumming his fingers on his desk. After a few minutes he gave up and went to his quarters. He needed to consider long and hard about the events of this day, and thought he could do it better here than at his headquarters. He got a bite to eat and then sat in his chair for a while, going over in his mind everything he knew.

***

While the Americans ate their supper, Tielson filled Drew and Dane in on everything he'd seen and discovered here, leaving out the confrontation with Zabronski.

"If I'm going to mingle with the

townspeople tomorrow, I'd better have a bath too. How about you, Shaw?" Drew asked.

"No, I'll wait until morning," Dane decided. "I'd better set the guard," he went on. "I'll take the first watch, Zabronski the second, Webster is third, and Fredericks fourth. Tielson, you get the night off," he smiled. Tielson grinned back.

Drew took off towards the pool. The others laid down, Angelique apart from the men, and Dane disappeared into the night. When Drew returned, he shivered from the cold air. But he felt good and clean from the warm bath.

Webster sat up. "Captain, it's getting chilly, can we get a fire going to warm us up?"

Drew looked around. "If we pile up some rocks so the flames won't be visible, I don't see why not." In a few minutes a fire spread its comfort and almost everyone fell asleep.

The lone exception being Angelique. She also desperately wanted a bath, but she wasn't about to take one with the remotest chance Zabronski might appear. She waited until she thought the others were asleep. She eased to her feet, and with the clean spare clothes and soap made her way to the pool. She undressed while shivering in the cool night air and slipped into the water. *Aah, it's so nice and warm. And it feels so good to be able to*

143

submerge my whole body under the water. The warm water soothed her aching muscles and she started feeling sleepy. She scrubbed her skin and submerged her body again. It felt so good to be clean. With reluctance she left the water, the cold air a shock to her body. As fast as possible she dried herself off and slipped on her clothes. Then a sixth sense warned her of a presence.

"Who's there?" she whispered.

A dark shape in the dark moved. "It's me," Dane's voice answered.

"You," squeaked Angelique, "You were watching me take a bath?" She felt outraged, betrayed and an unbelievable amount of hurt at the thought of him doing such a thing.

"No, I heard a noise and when I came to check it out, I realized you were in the pool. I didn't watch you take your bath; I looked all around making sure you were safe. I didn't see anything, I swear," he said with forceful conviction.

She relaxed, hearing the truth in his voice. They stood there, two blobs in the night. "Tell me about yourself, your family," she asked, wanting to know more about this fascinating man.

He shifted. "There's not much to tell. There's only my sister and myself. Four years ago, our parents were killed in a car accident. I was eighteen and Amy fourteen. Both of our parents were only children, so there aren't any uncles, aunts or cousins, and our grandparents had died by then. Since I was eighteen, the judge didn't put Amy into the orphanage and allowed me to become her guardian. She married early last year, and they're expecting their first baby."

A wistful tone crept into his voice. "I always wanted to go to West Point and become an army officer. I had the grades and wrote to my congressmen about an appointment. Things were looking good, but then the accident happened. I needed to take care of Amy and I couldn't if I went to school, so I dropped the request and searched for work. When Amy married, I volunteered."

She heard the longing in his voice.

He stirred again. "I've never told anyone else about my dream since..." He stopped, unable to continue.

"I am glad you told me, *mon* Dane," she replied, his wistful tone making her heart ache.

"I'm happy too," his voice dropping to a whisper. "I could fall in love with you, maybe I already am, I don't know. I only know you are very dear to me, Angelique."

"I could fall in love with you also, *mon chéri*." The night became charged with emotion.

Her breath caught in her throat as she swayed towards him.

"Why are you in Tunisia?" He broke the mood.

Strange, new feelings churned inside her. She didn't know if she was glad or sad he didn't try to kiss her.

Harshness came into her voice. "My family is from a town near Sedan. A *Boche* air raid killed Mama and Papa. We ran to Paris, and when the surrender came we fled to Marseilles. My brother needed to care for his wife and children, and they possessed little money. I heard about a teaching opening here in Tunisia. I applied and got it. I have been here for two years, teaching French and English to school children in Gafsa. When the *Boche* took over the country, the school closed and I have been trying to live ever since." Silence descended over the night again.

"Your religion is important to you," her voice became soft again.

"Not religion, my God is important to me," he disagreed. "I have a personal relationship with Jesus Christ, He's my Savior. He died on the cross and paid for my sins. He's the most important person in my life, and the One I want to obey and serve."

"I also believe in the Christ Child, but it is the Virgin Mary I must pray to. She is the Mother and Jesus must obey her."

"Why? Why do you say that, and why must He obey her?"

"It is what is taught to us. The priests tell us what the Bible says and we obey."

"Angelique, please read the Bible I gave you. All I ask is that you read it. Please say yes."

"If you want me to, I will try. I won't be able to understand, but I promise I will try to read it. It is a large book, where should I start?"

"Genesis, at the beginning of the Bible, is a good place to start. You can also read the Book of John."

They stood there a little longer. "*Monsieur* Drew wants me to go to Sfax, but I am so frightened." She shivered. "I am always so scared. Sometimes I am terrified of my own shadow. I wish I could be brave like you and him."

"We're scared too, Angelique. Anyone who isn't scared by what is going on is a fool. But," he groped for words, "it's something which has to be done. I rely on the Lord for help and guidance and the strength to face each challenge. Then I do the best I can. But the fear is always there. You can't let it master you, you have to control it. Sometimes you

147

have to do it a minute at a time. Just get through this minute, and don't worry about the next moment."

"Thank you, *mon chéri*, I will try to do what you suggest." She shivered again, from the temperature this time. "It is getting cold now, isn't it?" she asked.

At once Dane became all solicitous care for her and slung his coat over her shoulders. "Here, let's go back to the camp before you freeze."

She reached out and took his hand. They walked back up and around the hill.

***

As they walked, the tingle of their joined hands spread up Dane's arm. He thought about the conversation they'd shared. He thought he could have reached out, taken her in his arms and kissed her, and she would not have objected.

But he couldn't.

Kisses are for a husband and wife, and we aren't married. I can't ask her to marry me. I know from the bottom of my heart a born again Christian can't marry someone who hasn't accepted Jesus as their savior. She admitted she's never taken the step of faith and believed in Him. Lord, you know I've never been in love before. I'm pretty sure I'm falling head-over-heels for Angelique. If she wants me to kiss her, doesn't it mean she's in love with me? If two people are in love, shouldn't they get married? I'm so confused and mixed up.

Dane braked to a stop. He saw the glow of the fire reflecting off the wall behind the camp. "What in blazes?" He took off running to the camp, and since her hand in his remained attached to her body, she perforce ran too. "What's going on here?" he roared, kicking dirt onto the fire.

"What?" voices were heard as startled heads popped up.

"Corporal Shaw, what's the meaning of this?" Drew jumped to his feet. When Dane swung around to face him, Drew recoiled from the savage look on the other man's face. It must have been a trick of the firelight, but it seemed to the captain Dane's eyes reflected green.

"The light, it can be seen for miles," Dane stormed at him.

Drew looked at the fire. "Nonsense, the flames are well below the top of the rocks. They couldn't be seen."

Dane pointed to the wall behind them. "The reflection, it can be seen out there."

"Oh," Drew's face fell. "Maybe no one saw it." Even to him his words sounded weak.

"Captain, sir, this fire undid the false trail we laid down. Those Arabs must have seen the glow and they will come. We have to leave here now," Dane's adamant voice beat at his listeners like a tsunami.

"Shaw, let's not be hasty, let's think this through before we act," the captain soothed.

"Sir, if we leave here now and I'm wrong about the Arabs, we'll only lose an hour or two of sleep. But if I'm right, it'll save our lives. I made one mistake which might sign our death warrants. I'm not going to make a second."

For the second time Drew saw a look of total determination on the corporal's face. He realized Shaw possessed a streak in his nature which would never surrender, would never give up, would fight on to his last gasp and his last ounce of strength.

Drew wavered. He wanted to assert his authority, but the corporal's arguments were too logical and sound. Drew squared his jaw. He refused to jeopardize the mission over a petty argument over authority. "Pack up, we leave in five minutes," he ordered, with a newfound air of authority. With muttered grumbles and oaths, the men got up and started packing.

Nobody noticed Angelique's reaction to the confrontation. As the argument swirled, she shrank away, her eyes glued on Dane with a look of shock.

How could a man be so kind, so tender, so gentle one minute, and the next be so raging, so savage, so ...so...so untamed. She remembered the Arab with the knife Dane killed with such speed and ease. She began to perceive the hidden depths in the man, depths which frightened her.

Everyone raced around, and within the allotted time they were all packed and ready to go. Dane took a last look around and smothered the fire. Drew opened his mouth to make a suggestion, realized the reason for Shaw's action, and shut his mouth.

As they started walking, Webster asked Tielson, "Why don't we leave the fire burning? If the Arabs are on the way, won't it draw them there?"

Tielson glanced at him. "It'll take them longer to find the camp, which gives us more time to make our escape."

About an hour later shapes flitted in the darkness. On silent feet the intruders made their way towards the abandoned American camp. Hearing and seeing nothing, the Arabs realized their prey had flown. As they stood and looked around at the abandoned camp, the bearded leader grunted, "One of them is as sly as a fox."

"Shall we follow them?" the youngest and

least experienced raider asked, eager for murder and plunder.

"How, son of a donkey?" asked the leader, pointing to the forming clouds overhead. As he spoke, the first sprinkles spattered the ground. Within fifteen minutes pouring rain washed out all sign of the party's passing.

The American's were readying their new camp when the rain began. The cold downpour made them all miserable.

Dane counted it a blessing.

Chapter Nineteen

Major Lindisl woke up the morning of February 3rd. Taking his time, he ate his usual substantial breakfast and went to his office. A furrow between his brows marked his mood, which his underlings knew meant trouble for someone. When he entered the office, there were the normal standing-at-attention, heel-clicking, *Heil* Hitler salutes, to which he responded. He went to his office, and a few minutes later Captain Heidelstrauss, his second-in-command, knocked on the door with a fistful of papers.

"Since you've been gone a week, there's much to go over," Heidelstrauss said with a nervous look at his superior. To his relief, Lindisl nodded and held out his hand for the first report.

As Heidelstrauss handed it over, he said, "We picked up a handful of Jews."

Lindisl scanned and then signed their death warrants. "Stinking Jews, did they have any belongings?"

"No, *Herr* Major, only the clothes on their backs."

The next report told about a suspected Allied sympathizer being detained and questioned.

"*Herr* Major, either he was too stubborn to talk, or he actually knew nothing."

Lindisl noticed the past tense. "Was the body disposed of?"

"*Jawohl, Herr* Major."

More reports followed these lines.

"Here is a report about the battle at Faid, *Herr* Major."

Lindisl glanced at it, and then turned a penetrating eye to his subordinate. "And why would I be interested in this?" he snapped.

The captain gave a quick answer. "The attacking force captured an Arab as he fled from a destroyed American vehicle. He invoked your name and they him sent here."

Lindisl studied the report with more care and saw the Arab's name. "Send him in at once."

"*Jawohl, Herr* Major." The captain scurried away. A few minutes later, he led the Arab into the room, who bowed to the major, "Your servant, *effendi*," and Lindisl looked into the sly face of Abu Mehouf.

***

The American party woke up and ate breakfast. Angelique avoided her usual place between Drew and Dane. This time she sat between Drew and Fredericks, much to the latter's pleasure.

She glanced at Dane's hurt and puzzled expression, then looked down at her food. Drew couldn't resist a gloating look at his rival.

During the meal, Zabronski asked, "Where did you ditch the halftrack?"

Dane gave a vague wave northward, his hand encompassing a ninety degree arc, "Up there." He didn't trust the Russian.

"Where are the three cases?"Zabronski cast a meaningful look to the other privates.

Dane looked surprised. "We ditched them too. After all, we can't carry them, can we?" The others saw the sense of it. Zabronski ground his teeth with frustration.

After the meal, Drew turned to Angelique, "I thought you and I can walk over to Sfax. I'll hide in the outskirts, while you go into the city, buy me a suit and bring it to me. Then you lead me to the café. Do you think you can do this?"

Angelique grew frightened. Now the time had come for her to do what she'd agreed upon, she didn't know if she could go through with it. She glanced at Drew, and then, almost against her will, to Dane, who gave her a reassuring smile.

"I know you can do it," Dane said. "I'll pray for you, both of you," and glanced at Drew.

Somehow, Angelique drew strength from

Dane's confidence. She nodded to Drew and tried to give him a brave smile, but it wobbled.

Drew pulled Dane aside and spoke a few words. Then Drew and Angelique picked their way on the two mile trek to Sfax, the rain having stopped overnight.

Dane studied their campsite and the surrounding countryside. "I don't like it here; it's too hard to defend. Let's see if we can find a better spot." Within half an hour they found a place where sometime in the past a flood washed out an overhang.

Webster studied the space. "Do you think it'll hold all of us? It looks pretty small."

Tielson answered, "Yeah, it's just big enough."

"And it'll keep us dry if or when it rains again," Dane added.

"I'm all for that," Fredericks exclaimed.

Dane surveyed the surroundings, then gave an approving nod. "There's a decent field of fire. This is a place we can defend. Search around and see if there's water anywhere near."

A little later Fredericks returned and said, "I found water less than a quarter mile away."

"Good. You take Zabronski and fill all the water containers. Tielson, you stand guard on top of the hill. From there, you can observe anybody approaching. Keep a sharp eye out for the captain and Angelique when they return from Sfax and direct them here," Dane ordered.

***

Back in Sfax, Lindisl slapped a meaty hand on the table. "I paid you money to offer to work with the Americans, and much more when you brought important information to me. Yet all you have is that you were to lead this American captain to this café to meet this *Monsieur* Gascoigne. Have you nothing else to add?"

"No, *effendi*, but I did convince the German commander to let the American flee and not pursue him," Abu groveled.

Lindisl nodded. "Yes, quick thinking on your part and wise of the commander to listen." Lindisl jotted down a note to commend the commander. Then Lindisl's brow furrowed as he pondered. "Did he have any other contacts, anybody he knows in Sfax?"

"No, *effendi*, there is no one else." Abu sounded firm on that point. "I learned when the colonel hired me to bring the captain here that he is all alone."

"I wonder," Lindisl mused out loud as a thought came to him. "I think I might have seen

157

evidence of the good captain, but he wasn't alone; there were half a dozen men with him." He glared at the Arab. "How do you account for that?"

Abu raised helpless arms. "I don't know, *effendi*, maybe he picked up some stragglers from the battle?"

Major Lindisl gave a slow nod. "A possibility, yes." He felt excitement mount up in him. This could be the break he needed. There couldn't be two parties of American soldiers wandering around Sfax. This must be the group who stole his money. He needed to locate and capture them. He made a decision and pushed the buzzer on his desk.

When Captain Heidelstrauss entered, Lindisl spoke in German, "Establish an observation post to watch the *Le Belle Francaise Café*. This dog can identify an American spy who is to meet a Frenchman named Gascoigne there. When they are identified, have them arrested, but they must not be killed. I must interrogate them myself. Make sure you get both of them."

"*Jawohl, Herr* Major."

Abu lowered his eyes. He understood more German than the others suspected.

Chapter Twenty

As Angelique and Drew made their way towards the city, he frowned. "I must remember to speak only French when we reach town."

Angelique responded, "Why not start now? Let's make a rule; once we leave the camp we must speak French."

Drew smiled at her. "Good idea." They walked for several minutes while Drew searched his brain for something to talk about.

"Why are you in the army?" Angelique broke the silence.

Drew shrugged his shoulders. "My father was an officer and fought in the Great War. He wanted me to follow in his footsteps and join the army too. I went along with him. He got me into West Point and I graduated, not too high in my class, though" with a rueful look. He became animated. "I enjoyed learning Spanish and French, and once I spent an entire leave in France. I liked being in a foreign country and learning about the people and their customs " He looked at Angelique. "Your country has such a long and beautiful history, I really enjoyed it." He went on with his story. "After we entered the war, my fluency in French

159

became in demand, and they assigned me to intelligence."

"*Merci*, I am glad you like my country." Her mind went off on a sudden tangent. "I wonder if Dane ever visited France."

"Humph," Drew grunted, in a huff at the mention of the corporal. "Since he doesn't speak French, I doubt it."

Angelique pondered the difference in the two men. One who so wanted to become an officer but circumstances made it impossible, and the other who drifted along with his father's wishes and became one. And yet the one not an officer made most of the decisions, and the other seemed jealous.

"Have you seen all those places in your country you told me about yesterday?" She tried to cajole him out of his bad humor.

"Yes, my father became a career officer and we moved around a lot. The army assigned him to most of the bases in the U.S., but he only went overseas during the war."

They continued talking until they reached Sfax after mid-morning. When they were as close as they dared, Drew found a hiding place. "Now remember, find a shop which sells suits. I wear a size 38. Here is some money. When you walk towards the city be sure to look behind you so you can see the way back here. The land features look different when you are looking in the opposite direction, so be careful you don't get lost. Do you have any questions?"

"*Mon ami,*"she stared at him, confusion rampant on her face. "38 is a child's size. You're much bigger than that."

"What? You mean the French have different sized clothing than we do?"

She spread her hands. "It must be so."

"Great." He rubbed his chin. "What size would you guess I am?"

He looked so helpless. For some reason, his look of male ineptitude made her giggle and then break out in laughter. Her contagious mirth set him off and he joined in with her amusement. When they were able to stop and catch their breath, Angelique said, "I can't remember the last time I laughed like that."

"You should laugh every day," Drew said with a tender expression. They looked at each other, and then embarrassed, looked away. "I still don't know what size I wear," Drew said in a plaintive tone.

Angelique giggled again, and then composed herself. She looked him up and down. "My brother wears a size 44, and Papa," she choked

161

and then forced herself to continue, "Papa wore a 46. You are a little taller than them, so maybe a 48."

"Okay then," he squeezed her hand. "Go, and be careful."

"You too, *mon ami*," she took a deep breath and started walking. She strolled into town and mingled with the pedestrians. She remembered where some shops were located. Not wanting to draw attention to herself by asking a passerby for the nearest men's store, she made her way to the area she knew. When she got there, she meandered up the street, reading the names of the stores. After traveling down a couple of blocks, she spotted a likely shop. She halted outside the door, fear overtaking her. Up until now, she could walk away and no one would know of her presence. But if she entered the shop, she was committing herself to the operation, for better or for worse. "Oh Mother Mary, help me," she breathed, opened the door and walked in.

Once inside, she paused until her eyes became accustomed to the dark interior. She became aware of shelves and piles of clothes about her.

"May I assist you?" a polite voice in French spoke from the gloom. A little old man came into view, peering at her in surprise.

162

"*Oui,* I need a suit, please."

'I'm sorry, *mademoiselle,* but I only sell men's clothes."

She blushed. "I need a man's suit, *monsieur.*" At his continued look of surprise, she hurried on, "It... it's for my grandfather, to be buried in."

At once he became solicitous, and with sympathetic clucks directed her to the suits. "What size are you looking for?"

"48," she replied. *I hope it's correct,* she thought with inward trepidation.

"And for the funeral, it must be black," the little shopkeeper stated. With the air of a magician pulling a rabbit out of his hat, he produced a suit from a stack of clothes.

She held them up. They seemed the right fit. "*Oui,* I'll purchase this."

"How about a shirt? We have some nice ones here," he mentioned.

Her heart froze. They'd forgotten all about a shirt, and what about shoes and socks? He couldn't wear his army boots into town. *Oh what should I do?* she wondered.

Then she felt calm descend upon her, like a presence wrapping its arms around her. She remembered Dane said he would pray for her, and it seemed she almost heard his voice. She straightened her back. "*Oui*, I almost forgot. Also a shirt and a pair of socks, all of his have holes in them. One cannot be buried with holes in his socks."

The old man chuckled and busied himself gathering the items. "There must be a handkerchief, to be folded in his pocket, and a pair of shoes."

She remembered their footprints in the sand and how much longer his were than hers. "His shoes are this long," she held up her hands, showing the length.

The shopkeeper frowned at her hands, and then dove down and produced a pair of used, clean shoes. She made her purchases, and with the old man's condolences in her ears, made her way back to where Drew waited for her.

Drew whistled when he saw her packages. "What did you do, buy out the store?" he teased. Then he grew serious when she pulled out her purchases. "I never thought about those things," he groaned. "You make a better undercover agent than me," he said, bitterness at his shortcomings tinging his voice. Then he looked at her with respect and approval. "Thanks to your foresight we can proceed and find the café." He held up the pants to measure them against his legs.

"I'm not sure you should congratulate me,"

she said with a furrowed brow. She recounted her feeling in the store about a presence. "Do you think there's something to this God of Dane's?"

Drew stopped looking at the clothes. "I am not sure. He said some things which make me wonder if he is one of the wisest people I ever met, or maybe he does have Divine help."

"How long have you known him?"

He gave her a crooked grin. "One day longer than you."

"Oh." Astonishment splashed across her face. "What do you think about him?"

He paused, surprised at her question. After a moment of reflection he said, "I think it would be an honor to call him 'friend', but he would make a very dangerous enemy." His answer amazed him because he hadn't thought about the corporal in those terms before. He'd been more concerned about the impressions both of them were making on Angelique, topped with worry about his mission. But when he considered the other man, something convinced him his answer to be correct.

She shivered. "I think I know what you mean."

He gave her a penetrating look, wondering how deep her feelings were for Shaw, and then looked shamefaced. "I should never have said what

I did about him never being in France. It was petty of me. Please forget what I said."

She looked up into his face. *He's a big enough man to admit when he did something wrong.* The thought pleased her. She smiled at him and said, "I have."

He returned her smile and made a circling motion with his finger. "Turn around so I can get dressed."

"Oh," she said, blushing, and turned her back to him.

When he'd changed his clothes, he read his identification papers again to refresh his memory. Then he offered her the crook of his arm, "May I take you out to lunch, *mademoiselle?*"

She linked her arm with his and giggled, "*Oui, monsieur.*" They started walking back to town.

Chapter Twenty-One

Back at the camp, Dane squatted by the fire holding a cup of coffee in his hands. Zabronski ambled up to the fire and Dane looked up at him, "Tielson needs relieved, go take his place on guard duty."

"No."

Dane froze. "What did you say?"

"I said no. Someone else can take my shift, I'm not feeling good." Zabronski gave an insolent grin.

As Dane rose to his feet, his mouth went dry. The Russian chose an excellent time to challenge Dane's authority. The captain and Tielson, both of whom Dane knew would back him, weren't here. He could expect no help from Webster or Fredericks, who were awed by the big man.

Dane looked his opponent over. He was the biggest man Dane ever faced before. Zabronski stood about six feet tall and weighed around 200 pounds. He'd given Dane an out to back down, but Dane rejected it. If he accepted the flimsy excuse, he wouldn't be able to command any of the men again.

167

Dane felt the feeling welling up from deep inside him. The determination he would never give up, he would never surrender, he would keep fighting to his dying breath. With it came the other feeling, the one which frightened him to the core of his being. Rage, killing rage, which made him afraid if it ever escaped the iron hold he kept on it, he would kill, and kill, and keep on killing until everyone around him lay dead.

Zabronski's sneer left his face as the corporal's expression changed. Zabronski saw his opponent's face harden and a savage look come over it. Green flecks in the man's eyes begin to glow; a vision which both startled and touched Zabronski's heart with fear.

As Dane glided towards Zabronski on cat's feet, he felt a wave of deadly menace emanate from the smaller man which struck like a blow, The force of it backed Zabronski up a step.

Dane came up close to Zabronski and glared at him, trying by force of will alone to make the bigger man submit to him. "You will obey my orders, and you will go on guard duty now."

Fredericks and Webster watched the contest of wills going on.

Zabronski hesitated, started to turn away, then planted his left foot, and with a speed remarkable in such a big man, swung a huge fist at the corporal. Zabronski knew the power behind the blow. When it landed on the other man's chin, the fight would be over. Either the corporal would be knocked unconscious or slammed to the ground. And Zabronski knew what to do with a fallen opponent.

He missed.

With blinding speed Dane ducked under the blow. With the blazing quickness of a striking cobra he smashed two powerful blows into Zabronski's midsection. The first caused a grunt from the big man. The second knocked the wind out of him. Dane spun and kicked the back of the knee of Zabronshki's planted foot. As it buckled and the big man started going down, Dane smashed a karate chop into his throat. Zabronski hit the ground on his hands and knees, gagging. The fight lasted maybe three seconds.

The onlookers gaped at the speed and savagery of the onslaught. As Zabronski tried to suck air back into his lungs, he felt fear of a man for the first time since he was sixteen. He'd never been put to the ground so fast and with such ease in his life. He'd never seen anyone as fast as this corporal. The power in those blows shocked him. As he struggled to his feet, he saw the other man looking just as determined and just as deadly as before.

"Now, get on guard duty," Dane ordered, fire flashing from his green eyes.

Zabronski bent over and picked up his rifle. For a second he toyed with an idea. One look at the figure before him and he knew, without a shadow of a doubt, he would never get the round off, and then he would die. He walked up the hill with black hatred in his heart.

As the Russian walked away, Dane felt adrenalin leaving him, and as usual felt shaken. He half squatted, half fell, back down by the fire and picked up his coffee cup. To the others it looked like he remained unaffected by what happened. They looked at him with even more awe.

A few minutes later Dane remembered he'd promised to pray for Angelique. He felt an urgent, pressing need to pray. He got on his knees. "Oh Lord, I don't know what's going on right now. I beg you to protect her, give her wisdom if she needs to make a decision or what she needs to do." He poured out his heart to God, and after a few minutes the need left him, for a while anyway.

Chapter Twenty-Two

A little before noon, Major Lindisl eased himself into the room where his men kept watch on the café across the street. Three German soldiers saluted and Abu bowed to the major. "Well, any luck?" Lindisl demanded.

"*Nein, Herr* Major," reported the senior member of the party. "Do you know what description this *dumkopff* told us?" He went on, parroting the Arab. "Tall, but not too tall, slim and with brown hair. We've seen twenty men fit his description."

Lindisl motioned to Abu, who left the window and approached his master. "Don't you have any better description than what you told them?" Major Lindisl questioned in French.

"No, *effendi*, he is a most unassuming person."

Lindisl scowled as he pondered the Americans possible movements. They departed with his belongings yesterday morning. They might not have arrived yet, but with the halftrack they should have. "Does the café have a back door?" he queried in German.

The three soldiers looked at him with blank

stares. "I don't know, *Herr* Major," one of them said. "If he does try to enter there, wouldn't it draw attention to him?"

"Not if nobody is watching, *dumkopff*," Lindisl roared, furious at the ineptitude being shown. "Go and check if there is a back door." The German scurried out the door. Lindisl glared after him, wishing his *Gestapo* men were with him instead of having to rely on stupid German soldiers to do his work.

Meanwhile, one of the Germans kept an eye on the street, glad he wasn't the object of the major's wrath. He saw a couple, an attractive woman with black hair, and a somewhat taller man, slim, and with brown hair, come around the corner and walk down the street. He almost called to Abu to come and see the man. Then he thought the spy couldn't possibly be with a woman. The couple arrived at the café. When they saw all the outside tables were filled, they walked into the café.

***

Once inside, Drew and Angelique spotted a few vacant tables and sat down at one. Drew let his gaze wander around the room, and saw to his dismay three Germans at another table. There were a number of diners, most of them French, and a middle aged waitress who seemed to handle all the serving. He turned his gaze back to Angelique, who looked uncomfortable. "Relax, and enjoy the company of a handsome man and food you didn't prepare yourself," he said with a grin. She gave a trembling smile back, but did relax a little.

"I'm surprised I remembered the way here so well," Angelique announced. "I only came here twice with some acquaintances".

"Anyone special?" Drew asked with a teasing smile.

"No," Angelique smiled back. She added in a serious tone, "They were the couple I thought of asking if I could stay with when you found me."

Drew reached out and squeezed her hand in sympathy. "What kind of food do they serve here?" he asked, returning to more mundane matters.

"They're known for their fresh fish."

The waitress arrived with a large plate of different kinds of fish. "Welcome to *Le Belle Francaise,* what kind of fish do you desire, or do you wish for something else?" she asked.

"Fish is fine," Drew answered. He and Angelique made their choices and the waitress hurried to the kitchen to have them grilled. She returned and placed a bottle of wine with two glasses on the table.

"*Merci,*" Drew thanked her and poured the

wine.

"Now what should we talk about?" He leaned forward.

"How about your home in France?" teased Angelique.

"Gefosse-Fontenay? It's a small village on the Normandy coast, a nice place to visit," he answered.

"Did you make it up?" she asked, laughing.

"Oh, no, it's a real place. As a matter of fact, I became friends with some fishermen who lived near there and they took me out with them once." He sighed as he reminisced. "We went out and fished all night. I became soaked, the work exhausted me and I would hate to do it all my life. But I had a blast." He wrapped his hands around his wine glass, giving a pensive stare at the liquid. "I wonder what became of them," he muttered.

He gave himself a surreptitious shake and came back to the matter at hand: how to meet *Monsieur* Gascoigne. Drew glanced around the room, but nobody seemed to be paying any attention to them.

After a bit, the waitress brought their food, and they started to eat. There was a stir at the doorway and Angelique glanced up. All the color disappeared from her face.

Major Lindisl stood at the door.

***

When the German soldier returned to the lookout room, he dragged his feet and hung his head. *"Jawohl, Herr* Major, there is a back way."

Lindisl glared at the unhappy soldier while trying to keep from killing this idiot. "Get on the radio and call for another team to watch the rear exit. Then go back and keep an eye on it until they arrive," Lindisl gritted from between his teeth. He scowled out the window. "You three keep watch here; I'll go and have a look in the café." He left the room, strode across the street and into the building.

When he walked in, he looked around at the diners and started to sit at a vacant table. Then he saw a white-faced woman staring at him. He stared back at her, and then looked at her companion. His pulse beat faster. The man, slim and brown-haired, fit Abu's description.

Lindisl got up and marched over to their table, watching as her eyes got bigger.

"What is it?" Drew whispered when he saw the fright on her face.

"It's Major Lindisl of the *Gestapo* and he's coming this way," she whispered back.

Realizing because of her reaction, Drew needed to have one also, he turned and looked at the

175

blocky figure advancing towards them.

"Your papers," Lindisl held out his hand to them. Trembling, Angelique handed hers over, while Drew fished his out of a pocket and gave them to the major.

Lindisl glanced at hers, but scrutinized the man's. "What is your name?" he asked in French.

"Etienne Pinochet."

"Where are you from?"

"Gefosse-Fontenay."

"Gefosse-Fontenay? I have been there. A little village with a church with a beautiful stained glass window. The church sits in the middle of the town." When Lindisl worked in northern France, he'd passed by that particular village several times.

Drew looked up at him. His face remained calm, but his heart pounded. Out of the corner of his eye he noticed poor Angelique looked about to faint. "The major must be mistaken. Gefosse-Fontenay does not have a church in the middle of town nor a stained glass window."

"You know who I am?" Lindisl snapped. The man's answer about the church proved his familiarity about the village.

Drew gestured towards Angelique. "My…friend…has seen you before." He allowed some of the stress he felt to show. It would not do to act unafraid of the *Gestapo.*

Lindisl stood there, slapping the credentials into his free hand. Suspicion ran rampant in his mind, but he didn't quite know of what. He read the man's ID again. While he acted as if making idle conversation, Lindisl said in English, "Your French is very good."

By a supreme effort Drew kept his expression blank. *"Monsieur?"* Drew asked with a puzzled look. He heard Angelique gasp.

Lindisl whirled to face her. "You understood me?" he demanded.

"Oui, monsieur. I, I teach French and English to children," she stammered.

Lindisl scrutinized their identifications again. "What is your...friend's...occupation?" he asked her in English.

Angelique's mind went blank. She couldn't think. She pleaded, *Mother Mary, help me.* She couldn't remember. She watched as suspicion filled the major's face. Any second now she feared he'd haul them off for questioning.

Drew stared with a blank expression at the tableau, pretending not to understand.

Oh, the God of Dane, if you are real, help me, she prayed a quick and fervent prayer. The first she'd ever done to anyone else other than Mary.

Angelique opened her mouth. "He is a produce exporter."

Lindisl stared at both of them for a long minute. Both of them trembled as they waited for judgement. At last he handed their ID's back before returning his table.

Drew reached across the table and held her shaking hands. "*Magnifique,*" he breathed. She started to get up but he stopped her. "We cannot leave now or he'll get even more suspicious. We have to eat our meal."

"How can I eat now, after this?" she entreated, with huge frightened eyes.

Drew searched his mind for ways to relax her. "Let me tell you about my vacation a few years ago. After I graduated, I took a leave of absence and went to France on a holiday for a whole month. I landed at the port city of Brest and spent a couple of days there. Then I took the train to the town of Isigny in Normandy and spent a week seeing the sights. I rented a bicycle and pedaled around to several of the villages nearby, including Gefosse-Fontenay. That is where I met some fishermen and got acquainted with them. Then I took another train to Saint Mihiel where Dad fought. I stayed there for a while, biking around and visiting the places he talked about." Drew didn't think it necessary to mention the flirty and very vivacious *mademoiselle* he met and spent a lot of time with. "Then I stayed in Paris for a few days and went back to Brest where I caught the ship back home." Her returning color made her look more natural so he asked her, "Now tell me about your home."

She gathered her thoughts and started talking about a happier time. "I grew up in the town of La Budille outside of Sedan with my brother Louis. Papa taught at the school. That's where I learned English. Louis is two years older than me. He hated school but I enjoyed it. I loved learning about new things, the mental challenges." Her black eyes glowed with remembering the happiness of her childhood. Then she shook herself with a look of self-disgust. "I was too scared to go out and learn. I wanted the safety of the schoolroom."

"You did leave and come to Tunisia," Drew interrupted.

"*Oui*, it's the one time I ever did anything brave," she confessed. "Louis married the belle of La Budille, and he and Suzanne have two children. When we moved to Marseille, Louis only found common laborer jobs. There were too many displaced people looking for too few jobs. So," she shrugged her shoulders with a fatalistic attitude, "I needed to find some income. The man hiring for the job at Gafsa knew something of my father's academic standing and employed me. And now here I am, for better or worse." She shuddered and Drew reached for her hand again.

"You were courageous to come all this way by yourself," he said to encourage her as he squeezed her fingers.

She gave a wry smile. *I wonder what will become of me after these Americans leave Sfax?* Thrusting the thought away as too horrible to contemplate, her mind went off in a different direction. "I wonder if Dane is safe?" she asked with a worried look.

Drew felt the jab of jealousy. *Must she always be thinking of him?* He pushed the feeling away and concentrated on cheering her up. "I'm sure he is, they have a safe hidey-hole." He forbore to mention they were in much greater danger than the corporal.

Angelique giggled. "Hidey-hole?"

"Yes, it is a place to hide and be safe." He concentrated on cheering her up, and succeeded in sidetracking her mind with some funny recollections from his visit to France. Most of them consisted of gaffes he'd made which embarrassed him at the time. With relief he saw the sparkle return to her beautiful eyes.

Time passed as they talked and laughed. Lindisl kept his eye on them for a while. It appeared to him they were engaging in a romance, so he concentrated on the other diners. There were at least three men who answered Abu's description. But nobody met any of them. When the last of the three left, Lindisl gave up and followed them out of the cafe. He would make sure there were no Germans in the café the next day. Maybe then the spy would show up.

Late in the afternoon Drew looked at his watch. "I do not think we can stay here any longer. We do not want to bring unwanted attention to ourselves. It is best if we leave." He paid the bill and they walked outside. As a horse drawn wagon passed by, they walked along beside it to the corner. The wagon hid them from Abu's sight. They were each unaware of the other's presence.

Chapter Twenty- Three

As Fredericks stood guard, he spotted the twin figures walking towards the old encampment. He scrambled down the hill and met them. "We've moved to another campsite," he reported. "We're over here now." He led them in the right direction. "You missed a dustup this morning," he told the captain with an eager voice.

"What happened?" snapped Drew, anxiety creasing his brow.

"Shaw and Zabronski fought. Well, it wasn't much of a fight. Shaw knocked Zabronski down and Zabronski couldn't get up" He shook his head, wonder widening his eyes, "I know the corporal is a good fighter, but I didn't realize how tough he is." Drew hurried to the camp with a worried frown.

When they reached the camp, Dane stepped forward to meet them, "Are you all right?" he asked, concern written all over his face. He looked at Angelique first, which Drew found understandable. "I had this intense feeling a couple of times I needed to pray for you," as Dane looked them over. Drew stared at Dane, but saw only concern in his expression. He glanced at Zabronski whose bland face revealed nothing.

"We met the local *Gestapo* chief but not our contact. I'll have to go back tomorrow," Drew answered. He added, "I need to talk to you." The two men moved off. "What happened between you and Zabronski?" Drew demanded.

Dane replied, "Fredericks told you." Dane took a deep breath. "Zabronski refused a direct order. I convinced him to obey it." Dane frowned and mused out loud, "I don't know if I'm going to have trouble with him in the future or not."

The answer didn't satisfy Drew. "Who threw the first punch?"

"He did."

Drew studied the smaller man, but saw no marks. "Where did he hit you?"

"He didn't."

Drew looked surprised, but said nothing more.

Dane waited a second. "Are both of you going back tomorrow?"

Drew looked at Angelique. "I don't think so. She had quite a shock today."

They wandered back to the group, and Drew told them about the encounter in the café. He looked at Dane, "You said you had an intense desire to pray for us a couple of times. When were they?"

Dane thought a moment. "The first time was

late in the morning."

Everyone heard Angelique draw in her breath. She leaned forward. "When did you say?"

Dane frowned in concentration. "Late morning, must have been about eleven."

Angelique leaned backward, wonder showing on her face. "I entered the shop about that time," and she told about her experience.

The other listeners stirred and looked at each other with uneasy eyes.

It became Drew's turn to lean forward. "What about the second time?"

"Around lunch time, a little after 1200 hours," Dane answered.

Drew and Angelique looked at each other in amazement. Drew said, "That's when Major Lindisl questioned us."

Angelique added, "And that was when I prayed to your God, and I remembered the answer to the *Boche's* question."

They all looked at each other.

Tielson moved, uncomfortable with the possible meaning of the conversation. "I'll start fixing supper if someone will round up some firewood."

"I'll get it," Dane volunteered, and rose to his feet.

Angelique remembered her promise to Dane. With the strange happenings of the day in her mind, she got out the Bible and started thumbing through it. Drew reached over and turned the pages to John. Both of their heads bent over the book.

Dane smiled when he brought some wood in and saw them.

When Tielson called, "Come and get it," the others joined him at the fire. Angelique hesitated a second before resuming her place between Drew and Dane. Dane smiled at her. When they finished the meal, Dane glanced at Zabronski. "Go relieve Fredericks so he can eat." Zabronski looked at the corporal from under his bushy eyebrows. Obedient to the command, he picked up his rifle and left. When he turned his head, Drew saw a bruise on the other man's throat.

Angelique cleaned up from the meal. While Fredericks ate she retrieved the Bible. "Dane, I don't understand this." She pointed to John chapter three. "What is this being born again?"

Dane took the Bible. "Everyone is born into a physical family, right? Everyone has an earthly mother and father."

"*Oui*," Angelique agreed and Drew nodded.

"To be born into God's spiritual family, you need to be born a different way, a spiritual way.

That's the second birth John is referring to. Here in verse 14: 'And as Moses lifted up the serpent in the wilderness, even so must the Son of man be lifted up.'

"The Son of man is Jesus Christ, and the lifting up is His death on the cross," Dane explained.

Dane read, "Verse 15 says 'That whosoever believeth in Him should not perish, but have everlasting life.'

Dane scanned the faces watching him. "This is not talking about physical death, but spiritual death, or eternal separation from God. Every single person who believes in the Lord Jesus Christ will have eternal life.

He returned to the Bible. "Verses 16 through 18 explain how this happens. 'For God so loved the world.'

Dane looked up. "This is talking about everyone: you, me, Captain Matthews, even Major Lindisl. God loves each one of us so much, and He loves everyone the same way."

At this Angelique's eyes grew big.

Dane resumed reading, "'That he gave his only begotten Son, that whosoever believeth in him should not perish, but have everlasting life.'

"This means God the Father sent God the

Son to die on the cross. Everyone who believes in Jesus Christ will not die spiritually but will live forever with him."

Webster broke in. "Nobody lives forever. Everyone dies sometime."

Dane nodded. "Physical death, yes, but human beings are eternal. Genesis chapter two, verse seven explains it. When God created Adam, God breathed into Adam the breath of life and he became a living soul. God didn't do it to the animals. When they die, they perish. Not us, we have an everlasting soul."

Webster subsided with a confused look on his face.

Dane continued reading verse 17, "'For God sent not his Son into the world to condemn the world; but that the world through him might be saved.'

"God didn't send Jesus to send people to hell. He came to save people from going there. Verse 18 begins 'He that believeth on him is not condemned.'

Dane expounded, "Anyone who believes in Jesus as their savior is not condemned to go to hell when they physically die.

"Verse 18 continues, 'He that believeth not is condemned already.' This means everyone who doesn't believe is already condemned to spending eternity in hell. The reason is contained in the last phrase of the verse, 'Because he hath not believed in the name of the only begotten Son of God.'

Dane looked at the group listening. "They are condemned because they don't believe in Jesus Christ." Dane leaned forward in his earnestness, willing them to understand. "Can't you see how simple this is?"

Drew and Angelique looked confused. Drew answered, "We believe Jesus did exist. Doesn't it mean we are one of the 'born again'?"

Dane answered, "The Bible says the demons know and tremble. Do you think demons are going to heaven?"

They shook their heads.

Dane continued, "The demons know there is a Jesus, they've seen Him. The difference is sin. Romans 3:23 says 'For all have sinned and come short of the glory of God.' It means each one of us, me included, have sinned, and because we're sinners, we cannot come to God. God hates sin. Sin must be punished by death. When Jesus died on the cross, because He is sinless God, He paid for the transgressions of every single man, woman and child who ever lived or ever will. When Jesus rose from the dead, he took His sacrifice to God the

Father to pay for everybody's sin. The blood he shed washes away all sin, but only if you accept it. He's alive right now, sitting at the right hand of the Father, making intercession for His people."

Drew said, "I've heard it said we're all God's children. So you're saying Jesus intervenes on everyone's behalf?"

Dane shook his head. "No. His children are only those who accept His sacrifice as atonement for their sins. To accept the offer of salvation, you must accept the fact you're a sinner. There's nothing you can do of your own merit to warrant salvation and you ask Jesus to forgive your sins and come into your heart."

Dane searched for words as he breathed a silent prayer for guidance. "You see, Jesus is alive, His grave is empty. He physically rose from the dead. It's what makes all the difference in the world. When I got saved and asked Jesus to come into my heart, he did. I feel Him, I commune with Him and we communicate." Dane clasped his hands over his heart and stared with earnest fervor at his hearers.

Tielson, Webster, and Fredericks wore blank looks. Dane realized they didn't understand what he said. Drew and Angelique's expressions revealed their struggle to comprehend. Neither of them

189

seemed to reject his words, just not understanding what he meant. Judging he'd said enough for now, Dane straightened up. "You go ahead and read some more; I'll get additional firewood."

Later, as he dropped an armful of wood, he noticed Angelique staring into the fire, her eyes wide and her face white. Divining she was remembering the frightening experiences she went through today, he squatted down beside her. Searching his mind for some way to divert her, he asked, "What's your brother like?"

"Oh, Louis?" Startled out of her thoughts, she looked at him. "He is handsome, charming and very funny. As a boy, if there was any mischief going on you could be sure he was in the middle of it." She giggled. "His son, Philippe, is like him. He'll get into trouble and then charm his way out of it. He keeps Louis and Suzanne on their toes." She smiled again in remembrance of past misdeeds. Dane felt relief to see the strain leave her face.

"And you, *mon chéri*, what is your sister like?" Angelique asked.

"Not much like me in temperament," Dane chuckled. "She's a chatterbox and will talk your arm and leg off."

Angelique frowned. "I do not understand.

"It means she talks almost non-stop," Dane

explained.

"Oh, I see," she nodded.

"She's also headstrong, but kind hearted. Her husband, Bill, keeps her in line." Dane smiled, thinking of them.

Angelique heard the affection in his voice. "Is he not in the army then?" she queried.

"No, he was born with a club foot. It's not bad, but enough so he's ineligible for the draft, much to Amy's relief."

Drew walked up to the fire. When he saw them conversing and enjcying themselves, jealousy stabbed his heart. "Corporal, the guard rotation needs to be set." His voice came out sharper than he desired.

Dane watched strain come back into Angelique's face at the other man's tone. Anger roiled inside of him at the captain for causing it. Dane clamped down on his emotions. *I must settle the issue before it gets worse. But getting into an argument would solve ncthing. I'm a corporal and he's a captain. There can only be one result of a passage of arms between us. Besides, it would cause Angelique more stress.* "Yes, sir," answered Dane as he rose to his feet. He moved away, trying to marshal his thoughts.

Drew followed him and said in a quieter

191

tone, "I haven't had guard duty today. I'll take the first watch."

Dane turned around to explain how tension between them upset Angelique. The ashamed look on the captain's face and his words revealed he regretted his actions. Dane relaxed. "Yes, sir. I'll take the second watch, Zabronski the third, and Fredericks the last one." Dane looked back at Angelique, drooping by the fire with a sad, pensive look on her face. "She had a bad time today, didn't she?" Dane asked.

"Yes, yes she did." Drew looked at her. "She's a trooper though, handled herself like…like," words failed him.

"We need to make sure she suffers no more stress than necessary. Her welfare is the most important thing, other than the mission." Dane stared at the taller man, trying to get his meaning across.

Drew caught the inflection in the look and started to feel his temper rise. Then he looked at Angelique's slumping figure and squared his jaw. "You're right," he whispered, "Angelique's wellbeing is more important than ours." He turned and walked away.

Chapter Twenty-Four

Angelique woke early the next morning. Still bemused with sleep, she tried to work out the date. *Um, the fourth? Yes, February fourth.* Her bed lay at the very back of the overhang. She turned her head and saw Drew and Dane sleeping between her and the opening. Her eyes grew damp at their protection of her, even in sleep. She'd felt the bristling between the two men ever since they'd met, more so on Drew's part than Dane's. She knew she caused the antagonism, even though she didn't mean to or desire it. But last night when they made their beds she noticed the tension missing. She witnessed a look pass between them, and somehow felt they were more concerned with her safety and peace of mind than with male dominance.

She also thought of what Dane talked about last evening, about the Bible. Sometimes it felt like she was on the verge of understanding something incredible, but each time it slipped away. She remembered a long ago dream which happened soon after her parents' deaths. She'd been somewhere with dark corridors and somewhere ahead of her shown a light. No matter how fast she ran, the light always stayed somewhere ahead of her as she traveled up and down dark and twisting corridors. Listening to Dane talk about being born again reminded her of the dream, running and trying to catch the meaning, but never quite achieving it.

Sunlight brightened the air. She rolled to her side to get up. She saw Dane's eyes open. She couldn't resist giving him a tender smile, and saw the response in his eyes which made her feel warm inside. She did some necessary things and then started fixing breakfast for the group. The others roused up, and then they ate together except for Fredericks, who remained on guard duty. She and Tielson looked over the food supply.

"Captain," Tielson reported, "If contact isn't made today, we'll have to somehow get more food."

"I see," Drew replied. He pursed his lips, trying to think of a plan. "Go relieve Fredericks so he can eat."

"Yes, sir, "Tielson replied and left. Drew caught Dane's eye. Obedient to the unspoken command, he joined Drew and Angelique. The three of them sat down together.

"Should I go with you again?" Angelique asked.

"There's no need, you can stay here and rest," Drew answered.

She preferred this answer, but when she

heard it, instead of relief she felt a prickle of unease.

Dane shifted, uncomfortable with the words, with a worried look on his face. "I agree with you, it's the logical answer, but," he paused, "it doesn't feel...right." He looked at both of them with a puzzled look on his face.

Drew also felt something. He didn't know if the uneasiness of the other two influenced him. He reexamined the question and answers and saw no fault in the logic, but....

Dane said, "Let's pray about it." He closed his eyes and said out loud, "Dear Lord, we're facing a dilemma and we need your wisdom. Captain Matthews needs to return to the café and it could be dangerous. Major Lindisl might be there again, or some other Germans. Should Angelique go with him? Or should she stay here? It makes more since for her to stay. Wait a minute, Lord, you answered our question. Thank you, my Lord and Savior." Dane opened his eyes and looked at them. "She has to go with you. From what you told me about Lindisl questioning you, if he sees you and not her, he could get suspicious."

The other two looked at him. Drew replied, "I agree with you. It sounds logical to me."

"My subconscious must have realized it too. It's why I felt uneasy about my staying here, even though I'd rather not go." Angelique gave a little shudder.

"You don't have to go, you can stay," Drew began.

"*Non,*" Angelique sat up straight. "It is needful for me to accompany you. I know it."

Drew and Angelique glanced at Dane then at each other. Both saw in each other's eyes the knowledge of something, or someone, directing this man.

They jumped when Tielson yelled from the hilltop, "Planes."

Everyone's heads snapped up, searching the heavens and Dane yelled "Where, which direction?"

"Northwest," Tielson called back.

"Into the overhang, everybody," Dane commanded. He took enough time to yell up to Tielson, "Hide," and then dove into cover with the others. They all held their breaths.

***

Flight Sergeant Steutsel led a flight of four Messerschmitt 109's when he saw some movement on the ground near Sfax. A second look netted him nothing. Intrigued, he circled back to take a closer look. Again he saw nothing. He gave a mental shrug. He reasoned it must have been some skulking Arab. There's no way there could be any enemy this far behind the lines. He flew south towards Gabes and the British positions to his patrol area, forgetting the incident.

***

After the planes left the American party rose from their hiding place and stared at the disappearing planes. "Are we safe?" Angelique asked, her voice trembling with fear.

Dane followed the departing aircraft with his eyes and said, "They flew back so they noticed something. They didn't fire so they didn't see us. They're continuing their flight so I don't think they called for ground back up, otherwise they would circle to mark our position. I think we're safe."

Angelique heaved a huge sigh of relief.

While they waited for the time to leave, Angelique pulled out the Bible and Drew moved over to sit beside her. She started to read out loud when Zabronski let out a loud curse, jumped to his feet and stomped away. Webster tittered and followed him while Tielson looked uncomfortable but stayed.

With sorrow in his heart, Dane watched them go. Angelique started reading again. She and Drew talked over the passages with Dane, asking questions. Both of them felt a drawing and a curiosity about the Word of God neither one ever felt before. After a while, Drew looked at his watch. "It's almost 1100 hours. It's time for us to go."

Angelique gulped, then stood up. "I'm ready."

Dane gave her an encouraging smile and the other two set off to Sfax.

As she walked beside Drew, she asked, "You said you just met Dane, how did you meet?" Drew explained about being assigned to contact someone at the café, his guide Abu Mehouf being killed when they ran into the tank column and his escaping from his burning vehicle. Then he described joining up with Zabronski (she shivered at the name) and Webster, and then with Shaw and his three men. Soon they arrived at Sfax and mingled with the other pedestrians.

Chapter Twenty-Five

All morning long, the same four men from the previous day were in the same room watching the comings and goings from the café across the street. The Germans were bored, and as they assumed Abu didn't understand German, started gossiping among themselves.

"I heard the money from the Jews never made it to the airport to be flown back to Germany," one of them said. The other two looked at him, waiting for more information.

Abu's ears twitched, but he kept his eyes glued to the street.

"I hear the major took a halftrack and some men out of town, and he returned without them," the first man went on with a knowing wink.

"Shush," one of the others looked worried. "If he hears this being bandied about, it's not all who's going to disappear." The other two men shut up with equal fearful expressions.

Abu's brain functioned with furious speed, digesting this information. A halftrack carrying a fortune waiting in the desert and guarded by a mere handful of men would be ripe for plucking. His eyes gleamed with avarice.

About an hour later, Abu watched a man down at the end of the street with the right build and brown hair of Captain Matthews, but Abu couldn't see his face. He pressed against the window, trying to see. At the same time, Angelique and Drew were walking from the opposite direction towards the café. Drew glanced around and saw an Arab's face in the window across from the café. As the Arab's head turned, Drew saw Abu. Drew froze for an instant. As possibilities raced through his mind, he turned his towards Angelique and whispered, "Look at me and laugh."

She complied in an instant. With a worried look in her eyes, she whispered back, "What's wrong?"

"We are being watched." As her eyes started to look around he hissed at her, "Keep looking at me. Now keep smiling until we get into the restaurant." He kept his face averted, facing her, until they entered the café. At the entrance they stopped with their backs to the street, and Drew checked the café out. There were no German uniforms in sight, and there were more patrons than yesterday. He studied the diners and tried to pick out possible undercover German agents. Although there were a handful of men who might fit the bill, they were all sitting with a family group or with old men. Drew felt sure, or as much as he could, there were no *Gestapo* agents in the café.

***

Across the street the French speaking German grabbed Abu by the neck and yanked him from the window. "*Dumkopff,* do you want to be spotted? Stay back from the window."

Abu swallowed his anger and looked out the window. He saw a couple disappear into the café. Abu narrowed his eyes. He caught a glimpse of the back of the male figure. Something about him reminded Abu about his quarry. No, how could the captain be with a woman? Abu went back to studying the street.

***

There remained one open table in the crowded café. Drew led Angelique to it and they sat down. She whispered again, "Who's watching us?"

Drew smiled back at her. "Remember the guide I told you about, Abu Mehouf? He is in the building across the street."

Angelique looked at him with horrified eyes. "You said the Germans killed him."

"Apparently they did not," Drew answered. He drummed his fingers on the table. "Now the question is, why is he sitting across the street watching the café?"

201

"He could be waiting for you to show up." Angelique suggested.

"He might, but why not sit out by the street? How many Arabs did we see standing or sitting around? No, he's trying to hide. Who is he hiding from, the Germans or me?" He rubbed his forehead, trying to think. *I need help. What's going on? If Corporal Shaw, Dane, were here, he'd pray. Will his God answer me?* He dropped his hand as a thought popped into his head.

The arrested look on her companion's face startled Angelique. "What is it?" she whispered.

"If Abu sold me out to the Germans, it would explain why I escaped, why they didn't chase me when we ran into the tank column. I'll bet Abu is watching the front door of the café to point me out."

"Why are they watching and waiting? Why not raid now?" Angelique asked with a nervous tic. Fear of what could be mounting in her.

"It is because they want to catch the informant. They do not know who it is, and they want me to lead them to him," Drew answered in bitter disgust.

"Do you think Major Lindisl being here yesterday is a part of it?"

"I expect so." Drew pressed his fingertips

together as he pondered. "I am thinking they did not have the surveillance set up yet, so he checked the place out. Remember how he came straight over to me? He must have been going by my description."

The waitress arrived at their table. "Ah, *Monsieur* and *Mademoiselle*, you've returned. You enjoyed our cuisine, yes?"

"Indeed we did," Drew answered with a pleasant tone, trying to act at ease. "And what delicacies do you have for us today?"

"Alas, only the same choices as yesterday," she answered with a sad expression. "But it's all fresh caught from last night. What would you desire?"

Angelique and Drew made their choices and she hurried away.

"If he recognized you, then they're watching us to see who the contact is. It's better for us to leave and never come back," Angelique returned to their conversation.

"I do not think he did, "Drew answered with a frown. "If he did know who I am, then he never would have approached me. After he returned to his table I noticed he kept his eye on some other men. Now I think of it, they fit my general description. Also, we cannot leave yet, we have not gotten the information." He looked over the room, irritation rasping his voice. "I wish we possessed a better organized way of making contact. We and the informant might be sitting around and waiting for the other one to initiate the meeting."

"And we could be all wrong in our suppositions, and Abu is waiting for you to appear," Angelique sighed.

***

Back at the camp, while Dane and Tielson were busy and Fredericks on guard, Zabronski cornered Webster. "I've been thinking about all that money," Zabronski began.

Webster looked around to make sure they couldn't be overheard. "Well, it's not going to do us any good, now is it? Only the corporal and captain know where it's at. And if we do get our hands on it, where would we go?"

"I've got it all planned out. When we pick up the halftrack, we take over. We drive to Algiers and hire one of those Arab boats to take us to Portugal, and then fly back to the States. Easy as pie."

Webster grimaced. "Easy as pie, huh? After what Shaw did to you without half trying, what makes you think you can get away with it?"

Zabronski's face turned ugly. "I've got plans for him too, and he won't get close enough to touch me either. I'll shoot him when he won't be expecting it and I'll leave him to die. Are you with me or not?"

Webster chewed on the idea. He remembered how the sight of all the wealth tempted him when he first saw it. "What about Angelique and the captain?"

"Oh, we'll turn them loose when we leave Algiers," Zabronski lied. He didn't intend to leave any witnesses. How long Angelique lived would depend entirely on how well she pleased him.

"Well, if you're sure it'll work. It would be real nice to have money for once in my life."

Chapter Twenty-Six

As Drew and Angelique ate their lunch, they avoided the subject uppermost in their minds—meeting the informant. Instead, Drew talked about his family: his parents and younger brother and sister. "Dad is a crusty career officer. He must be, oh, fifty-eight now. My mother is his second wife. His first wife died in childbirth, her and the baby both. It took him a while to recover from the tragedy. When he met my mother, he thought he was too old for her. When he told her, she looked him right in the eye and said, "You're the right age for me."" Drew and Angelique chuckled. "Now he is training troops back home."

"Mom is the organizer. She needed to be with so many moves in her lifetime. She keeps the home fires burning and all of us in line. Dad acts tough, but he would be lost without her."

The expression on his face and his voice told Angelique of his deep attachment to his mother. It brought an ache to her heart and a lump in her throat as she thought about her Mama and Papa.

"I am the oldest. David is three years younger and a lot like Dad, they bump heads a lot. It used to drive Mom nuts. Then she got so she would tell them to go outside, fight it out and not come in until they were ready to be peaceable." Drew shook his head in wonder. "She got their attention because neither of them wanted to upset her. Now because they aren't living in the same house, they get along with each other better.

"Betty is the youngest and the apple of Dad's eye." Drew chuckled again. "You ought to hear the third degree Dad gives her young men when they come to call. It used to make her upset until Dad told her he was waiting for the man who would look him in the eye and stand up to him. He'd be the man who would be worthy of her. That caught her attention, and the last letter I got from home sounded like she might have found one."

Angelique gave a puzzled smile. She liked hearing about his family, but she didn't understand some of the phraseology. "What do you mean about bump heads, nuts, apple and third degree? I don't understand what you mean."

Drew laughed and explained the idioms. Time flew past as they continued chatting.

They looked up in surprise at the almost empty café when the waitress stopped at their table. "Well, it's so nice to see young people enjoy themselves again," she heaved a big sigh. "Do you mind if I set down and rest my feet?"

"Of course not," they answered in unison.

She pulled up a chair. "Nowadays young men and women have no time to sit and be romantic with each other. It's all rushing about and looking behind them in fear lest they get clapped on their shoulders and arrested." She sighed and beamed at them.

Angelique gasped. She'd forgotten about the danger they faced while conversing with Drew. The dread of Major Lindisl arresting her hit like a blow in the solar plexus.

"Oh, to be back in the old days, sitting on the Left Bank, sipping wine, and flirting with all the young men. How long has it been since you've been in France?"

"Two years," Angelique answered. Drew didn't respond.

"I've been here in Tunisia for twenty years. My husband brought us here, and we opened this café. He named it after me, and we ran it together until he died two years ago. France's surrender crushed him; he was never the same afterwards." She sighed again with a faraway look in her eyes. "Do you know what I miss the most about France?" she asked in a dreamy tone. She went on without waiting for an answer. "The lilies. The lilies are beautiful by the Loire."

Drew froze.

He gulped, and then answered, "I prefer the lilies of Garonne."

She bent forward and Drew stared into shrewd brown eyes boring into his. "Who is she?" indicating Angelique.

"She is a long story, and the means of getting here. But," Drew looked confused. "I thought I was to meet a *Monsieur* Gascoigne?"

The waitress chuckled. "It puts a lot of people off." Then she grew serious. "You must get this information back to your people. General Arnim is going to attack near Sbeitla with the 10th and 21st Panzer Divisions within a few days."

"How do you know?" gasped Drew.

The woman's face grew cold. "My daughter's lover is a German officer. Sometimes he's indiscreet." At their looks of horror, she shrugged her shoulders. "One does what one is able," she said, her meaning obscure.

Drew became all business. "The café is being watched from across the street. I am not sure if the Germans are involved or not. Is there a back way out?"

Fright widened the woman's eyes. "If the Germans are watching the front, then they're watching the back also. What makes you think they're out there?"

Drew explained in rapid words. "So," she nodded, "you think they're searching for you so you'll lead them to the informant. If you try leaving by the back door, the Germans will of course be on to you and it will cause suspicion to fall on me. But if you leave by the front door like any other customer, you may get away if this Abu can't see your face. How can it be done?"

They all three pondered various stratagems, and then Drew got an idea. "Maybe if I use this handkerchief to wipe my face as I walk out, until I can turn away, maybe we can escape?"

The woman nodded. "Yes, it might work, and you can shade your face from the sun also."

Angelique sucked in her breath, remembering her conversation with the shopkeeper. On such a little thing like purchasing the handkerchief might decide whether or not they would escape. What made her agree to purchase the handkerchief? Or who? She shuddered.

"No time like the present, let's go." Drew stood up and pulled Angelique to her feet. "Thank you for the delicious meal, we shall return again," he announced in a louder voice and paid the bill. They walked to the door and he pulled out the handkerchief. As they stepped outside, he mopped his face. They turned and sauntered down the street.

***

Abu watched them leave, but didn't see the man's face. Something about him, though, stirred a chord of memory. Abu kept watching while he worried at it. Then it struck him. The man walked with a military bearing, like a soldier with straight shoulders. "That's him," Abu shouted. "That's Captain Matthews." At once two of the Germans rushed to the window and spotted their quarry, while the third got on the radio and called headquarters.

"We found the American," the radio man reported. "He and a woman companion have left the café and are walking down the street. What are your instructions?"

"Has he made contact with the spy?" asked the man on the other end.

"We don't know."

Back at headquarters Major Lindisl charged out of office when he heard the call and stood listening. "What are your orders, *Herr* Major?" the radio operator asked.

Lindisl thought for a second. He weighed in the balance the possibility of capturing the spy versus the certainty of regaining his lost money. "Raid the café with one man from the rear and two from the front. Send two men each from the front and rear to pick up the Americans. Bring them here at once."

The operator passed on the commands. Then he called the watchers at the rear to give them their orders and the description of the two.

Chapter Twenty-Seven

The first hint to Drew and Angelique of things going wrong happened when they passed the mouth of the alley which ran behind the café. Two men in civilian clothes emerged from the passageway and closed the distance between them with a fast walk.

"Halt," called one, and then in laborious French, "Come with us." Both Germans pulled pistols from their pockets.

The street emptied of passersby.

Drew turned and faced his challengers. "*Monsieurs?*" he asked, turning the palms of his hands upwards as if puzzled by the interruption.

The Germans waved their pistols for Drew and Angelique to proceed back towards the café.

Drew took a couple of steps forward and to the side so one German stood in front of the other. Drew burst into action. Springing forward, he slapped the nearest German's gun hand out of the way before he could react. Drew bunched his fist and landed a haymaker on his opponent's chin. The force of the blow knocked him backwards into the second German. His head slammed into the wall and he slumped down, unconscious. As the first

German started to get up, Drew kicked him in the jaw. Like his friend, this German also lost interest in the proceedings.

Drew snatched up a pistol and looked around. Ahead of him down the street he spotted a corner where another winding street intersected this one. Because of the angle, it offered hope for an escape. He heard feet running towards them. They were on the same side of the street as the café and the slant of the twisting avenue hid them from view for a few vital seconds.

Acting on a sudden urge, he grabbed Angelique's hand and sprinted towards the running feet. They ducked into the narrow, winding alley. A twist in the passage took them out of sight of the street. Drew pulled Angelique to a stop. They plastered themselves against the wall and listened to running feet pass by. Drew sagged in relief and gave Angelique a wavering smile.

Abu and the German with him raced around the bend. They braked to a stop when they saw their two companions struggling to their feet. Giving wild glances around at the vacant street, one of them pointed to the intersecting street ahead and exclaimed, "They must have gone that way."

Drew and Angelique heard the voices and feet recede as their pursuers continued on away from them. Drew pulled Angelique by the hand and traveled down the alley. When they reached the open back door to the café they paused. Raised voices and commotion from within told Drew the Germans were rounding up everyone inside. Drew peeked through the doorway. He didn't see anyone. They rushed past the door. When they reached the other end of the alley, they turned and hurried on down the street.

Behind them, Abu and the Germans ran down to the intersection. Two Germans sped on down the street, while Abu and the other German turned onto the side street. However, it became a dead end and they retreated back to the intersection, where they met the other two. Bewildered by the disappearance of the fugitives, they hurried back to the surveillance room to report in.

The Germans raiding the café fared no better luck. They questioned everyone inside the café, but didn't find any trace of a '*Monsieur* Gascoigne' and also reported in.

Furious, Major Lindisl snarled, "What do you mean you lost them, *dumkopff*?"

The lieutenant in charge at the surveillance gave an apologetic answer, "*Herr* Major, he knocked out the two men trying to arrest him, and then they disappeared."

"What about the spy? Was he apprehended?" Lindisl demanded.

"*Nein, Herr* Major. No one in the café is named *Monsieur* Gascoigne," replied the lieutenant, sweat drops of fear forming on his brow.

Lindisl drummed his fingers on the table. "You questioned everyone, I assume?"

"*Jawohl, Herr* Major. I have all the suspects. Do you want to see them?"

"*Ja*, bring all of them here, I will interrogate them myself. Meanwhile, and more important, catch that American." Lindisl slammed down the phone.

The lieutenant heaved a sigh of relief and wiped his forehead. Within minutes, the well-oiled German machine started sealing off the section of the city. Trucks roared out, dropping soldiers at key points to form a blockade. Teams of men worked up and down the streets, looking for the pair. Abu Mehouf joined one of the groups.

After Drew and Angelique made their escape, they started working their way west, getting their direction from the sun. But the streets were crooked and winding and they were in an area unfamiliar to Angelique. They were soon lost. The street they were on turned and wound more or less northward.

Up ahead of them they saw some kind of

disturbance. Peering ahead, Drew made out the shape of a German truck blocking the street. He cast a quick look around. "Here," indicating an intersecting street, "this way, this passage goes west." Angelique looked at it in distaste. The narrow route with trash littering the ground looked worse than the ones they'd so far traversed, but obedient to his instruction she turned into it. The way remained narrow and winding, and all the intersections were with constricted alleys. The looks they were getting from the few Arab passersby were not friendly. Drew got more and more worried as the street bent back the way they'd come.

Then three Arab men stepped out of an alley, barring their way. Brandishing knives, one of them said, "Your money, at once, French dog,"

Drew pushed Angelique behind him with one arm while he pulled out his pistol with the other hand. This gave the Arabs pause. Now they were in a stand-off. Drew didn't want to fire his gun to draw attention to themselves, and the Arabs lost their desire to rush him.

Angelique swiveled her head, looking for a way out, her heart in her mouth. Crowd noises came from a narrow alley next to her. She grabbed Drew's free arm, "This way." Angelique hurried down the alley, her shoulders almost touching the run-down buildings on each side. The smell from the garbage piled on the ground made her gag. Angelique tried to hold her breath as much as possible. She shuddered at what she must be walking through. Drew trailed behind keeping watch on the Arabs. They were disinclined to follow, contenting themselves with making threatening gestures with their knives.

Angelique turned a corner and found herself in a square. Drew shoved the pistol into a pocket. They started to walk to the other side, mingling with the other pedestrians. Halfway across, they saw to their horror German soldiers guarding the exits. Drew turned around and bumped into an Arab's back. The Arab turned around, and Drew looked into the face of Abu Mehouf.

Chapter Twenty-Eight

Shocked to see Captain Matthews right in front of him, Abu opened his mouth and shouted, "Here they are," instead of trying to inveigle his way into their confidence.

Drew threw a punch and knocked Abu down. The nearby Arabs, seeing a Frenchman hit one of their own for no apparent reason, started shouting imprecations and milled about him. The German guarding the nearest exit waded into the melee and used the butt of his rifle to clear a path for himself. The volatile Arabs then turned on him and a shoving, yelling, wild melee ensued. As more German soldiers entered the square, a group of Arabs and French rushed away down the unguarded street, sweeping Drew and Angelique with them. As they raced along, they saw a squad of Germans coming towards them. Some Arabs from the group split off and turned down a narrow, smelly alley. Drew and Angelique followed them. After a short distance they spilled out into a broader, cleaner street and everyone scattered.

Drew and Angelique dropped down into a saunter and made their way along the street. "Whew," Drew mopped his face. "That was close.

Well, at least we know which side Abu is on."

"Why, did you see him?" Angelique panted from the exertion of running.

"That is who I punched back there."

Angelique's eyes grew big, "*Mon Dieu,*" she gasped. As she gazed around, her mouth dropped open and she halted. "*Monsieur* Dupleix, *Monsieur* Dupleix," she called out. A balding, middle-aged man walking down the street looked around and saw her waving at him. She dashed to his side. Drew followed, wondering at her actions.

Monsieur Dupleix peered through his spectacles at her and then asked in wonder, "*Mademoiselle* DuBois?"

"*Oui,* it is I," she answered him, still panting after her exertions.

"Why my dear, what are you doing in Sfax? I thought you were in Gafsa." He beamed at her.

"I was, but when fighting broke out there I went to Faid and now I'm here."

"I'm on my way home now, please come with me. Mathilde would be pleased to see you," he invited them. He peered at Drew. "And who's this?"

"This is…," Angelique started to say and then stopped. She couldn't remember the name on Drew's ID.

"Etienne Pinochet, at your service." Drew

bowed to the older man, who with a smile acknowledged the greeting.

Theo Dupleix led them to his home while Drew explained how they happened to meet him. "We got caught up with a mob running away from some Germans and lost our way. Then *Mademoiselle* DuBois saw you."

Theo threw his hands up in the air, "Oh, those *Boche*." He looked around with a guilty expression and then continued his tirade all the way home. Drew hid a smile. To hear the Frenchman talk, one would think Germans were the cause of all the sins of the earth.

They arrived at the small abode of the Dupleix family and went in. "Mathilde, you'll never guess who I ran into," Theo announced as he entered the house.

"Who is it?" a feminine voice answered followed by the appearance of its owner, a plump woman who blinked at the unexpected guests. "Why, *Mademoiselle* DuBois, Angelique, whatever are you doing here?" she asked, eyes bulging with surprise.

So Angelique explained again how she happened to be in Sfax, leaving huge gaps in her story, such as how she got here. In response to Mathilde's unasked but obvious question she introduced Drew. After a few minutes chatter the Dupleix's went to get some refreshments. While they were absent, Angelique whispered to Drew, "Do you think we should leave now? I can find my way out of the city from here."

Drew considered and then shook his head, "Let us wait a bit for things to calm down."

Their hosts rejoined them with a dish of dates and a bottle of wine. Mathilde wasted no time in starting what she thought to be a subtle examination. "Where are you from, *Monsieur* Pinochet? I must say your accent is unfamiliar to me."

Drew tried not to look worried. "I am from Gefosse-Fontenay in Normandy."

She still looked puzzled. "Gefosse-Fontenay? I don't believe I've ever heard of the town. Where is it?"

"It is near to Isigny."

"Oh, Isigny, yes, I know where that is." Still not satisfied about his accent, she decided to ask a more pressing question. "How long have you and Angelique known each other?"

Rather nonplussed, Drew replied, "We met while traveling from Faid to Sfax."

"What were you doing in Faid?" as she passed him a glass of wine and offered the dates.

Drew took a sip of wine and a date while he tried to organize his thoughts. "I was looking for a source of fruit for exporting. I am a fruit exporter."

Theo took a date and a glass after serving Angelique. "What company do you work for?"

Drew choked on the date. He'd never thought about a name of a company and forgot his identification said freelancer. When he stopped coughing he muttered, "The Marseille Fruit Company."

Theo looked puzzled. "The Marseille Fruit Company? I don't believe I've heard of them."

"Oh, it is a new company, just starting. I am trying to line up some contacts," Drew stammered a little.

"Well, if you like I can point you to some local growers. I'm sure some of them may be interested if the price is right."

"Oh, thank you very much. I'm sure I'll be in touch with you in a day or two." Drew didn't quite know what to say and cast an anguished eye at Angelique.

She came to his rescue. "Oh, look at the time. We must leave before curfew."

"The curfew?" Theo exclaimed and went off on another tirade. "Those Germans are always interfering with us ordinary and peace-loving citizens." His face turned red with indignation. "Do you know what happened to me three days ago? A soldier stopped me on the street and demanded to see my papers."

When he ran out of breath Mathilde interjected, "Where are you off to?"

"We're staying with some people we met on the journey, and we must be on our way," Angelique set down the empty glass and rose to her feet, followed by Drew.

"Who are they? Perhaps we know them," Mathilde pressed, evident suspicion growing in her.

"I don't think so, they are new to the area, refugees also," Drew stumbled at the look his hostess gave him.

"Thank you so much for your hospitality, it's so nice to see you again," Angelique gushed as she led Drew to the door. Before the astonished couple could say any more, Angelique and Drew were gone.

"Whew," Drew sighed in relief. "I am so glad to get out of there. I am not sure what Madame Dupleix thought but I am sure it meant trouble." He looked at Angelique's flushed cheeks. "Why, what is it?"

Angelique flushed more. "I think she's suspicious I'm...entertaining. They're very moral people." Embarrassed, she couldn't go on.

Drew's mouth dropped open. "What? Well I never, oh." He shut his mouth, also embarrassed.

Gathering her composure, she indicated the direction they needed to go. "This way leads us out of the city."

Drew fell into step alongside of her. He thought about the events of the past hour. He burst out, "You know, we are having an incredible run of luck."

Angelique looked at him with an unfathomable look in her dark eyes. "Would you call this just plain 'luck'? We successfully enter and leave a café the Germans have under surveillance, at least once and maybe twice. When they try to arrest us, you knock two armed men out. When we are discovered again, a mob of Arabs interfere. When we follow a group running away, they lead us to one of the few people I know in this city. From their house, I know the way out of the city."

Arrested by her words, Drew stumbled. "It doesn't seem likely, does it? Either someone is leading us on, or..."

Angelique nodded. "Or someone is praying for us again."

Drew's mouth twisted. "You know, when we were discussing Abu in the café, I didn't know

225

what to think about him. I kind of prayed. That is when I thought about Abu being a traitor." Drew took two more steps. "And it turned out to be true."

Deep in thought and without another word, they walked on down the street which ran more or less westward, the direction they wanted to go.

They followed the street until it reached a large square with shops on the east side. On the west side stood an old city wall, punctured now in several places where streets went through to a built up area beyond. Through the gateway in front of them, they saw the street continuing through the houses and on out of the city. A German truck partially blocked the gate. A German soldier sat behind the wheel. When Drew looked around the square, he saw German sentries posted at each entrance. The couple melted back into the crowd.

"Now what do we do?" Drew breathed. He looked around for inspiration. He noticed the nearby shops: a coffee house, a bakery, what looked like a junk store, a grocery store, a shop selling women's hats. Something clicked in his head. "Angelique, get some white flour or something which will turn my hair white for a few minutes from the grocery store." He handed her a fistful of money and pushed her towards it. Not waiting to see if she obeyed, he went over to the junk shop and picked out a short walking stick about two feet long he'd noticed in the window. The proprietor wanted to haggle about the price, but Drew handed him a franc which left the man speechless.

He returned and saw Angelique leaving the grocery store with a small bag. He led her back down the street to the nearest ubiquitous alley. With quick words he explained his plan. Then Angelique covered his hair with white flour. It wouldn't withstand anything like an inspection. It didn't need to. Leaning over on the short walking stick and dragging one foot, the prematurely white-haired, half-crippled Frenchman made his painful way back up the street and across the square. The German driver gave him a once over and then returned to watching the crowd for an almost six foot tall, brown haired man trying to leave the city.

Drew crept around the truck. When hidden from the view of the other German sentries, he straightened up and pulled out his pistol. He jumped onto the running board, and with one hand pointed the gun at the driver and with the other held up a forefinger across his lips in the universal sign of silence. The driver, surprised by the sudden advent of the apparition, needed to make a quick decision. Either sound the alarm and receive a posthumous award for bravery, or surrender without making a fuss. He started to raise his hands. Drew motioned for him to keep his hands down. Drew opened the passenger door and gestured for the driver to slide out. As he got near, Drew hit him over the head with his pistol and knocked him out. Drew muttered, "It's a good thing he's wearing a hat and not a helmet."

Angelique, while waiting for the driver to disappear, noticed three children playing nearby. She walked over to them and knelt down. "*Enfants, bonjour.*"

The eldest looked shy and returned her greeting. The smallest stuck her thumb in her mouth and gazed at Angelique with round eyes.

"Would each of you like to earn a franc?"

"A whole franc? For each of us?" Their eyes grew big as the oldest asked the questions.

"*Oui*, a whole franc for each of you. Walk with me across the square to the truck and wait until the truck drives away. Then you can come back."

"*Oui, oui, oui*," they echoed. Angelique stood up and noticed the disappearance of the driver. She took the hands of the two smallest children and walked across the square. The sentries noticed her, of course. They weren't watching out for a mother of three so she got only the normal male appreciation. When she reached the truck, the white haired driver wearing the cap and shirt of a German soldier sat behind the wheel. Angelique paid off her guardians and slipped into the cab. It was a tight fit, trying to lie down on top of the unconscious, shirtless German, but Angelique managed to keep out of sight as Drew started the truck and drove away. The sentries gaped at the sight and wondered why the assigned driver, Hans, left.

When they were out of sight of town, they stopped and dumped the driver out. Then they took off towards the camp. As they drove along Drew jerked his head and whistled, "I never thought of it until now, but you could have stayed with the Dupleix's."

Angelique gave him a blank look. "I never thought of it either." She felt an awful lump in her throat at the thought of never seeing Dane or Drew again. As she bounced along in the truck, the refrain kept going around and around in her mind: Dane and Drew, Drew and Dane. She looked at Drew. Fear clamped down on her. *What's going to happen to me? Now he's got the information, would they leave me?* Not able to stand the suspense any more, she asked, "Drew, what will you do with me?"

"Do with you?" he repeated with surprise. "Why, take you with us back to our lines, unless you want to remain here?" he asked with an anxious, worried look on his face.

"Oh no," she replied, happy now. "I would like to go with you." She settled back in her seat. Dane and Drew, Drew and Dane went around and around again.

Chapter Twenty-Nine

As the afternoon wore on, Dane became more and more worried. He felt again a pressing need to pray for Angelique and Drew, and spent a lot of time talking to God. So much so he missed an important conversation.

Zabronski sidled up to Fredericks. "I've been thinking about all that money, going to waste out there."

Fredericks looked up at him, fear touching his heart. He'd seen what Shaw did to Zabronski, and also knew he was no Dane Shaw. "What about it? I suppose we'll pick up the halftrack on the way back and the captain will turn the money over to the authorities."

"What'll they do with it? Who's to say it won't disappear into some moneygrubbing hands that have less right to it than we do? After all, we're the ones who risked our lives to capture it," Zabronski said.

"Well," Fredericks twisted, uncomfortable with the conversation, "it's nothing to do with me. I know the corporal is going to turn it over, and you can't stop him. The captain and Tielson are on his side about it too. There's nothing you can do about

231

it."

The Russian's face turned dark at the jibe about the fight. "Things happen during battles, people die," he snapped and walked away. He left a man behind him, frightened, and not knowing what to do.

As midafternoon came, Dane took his turn on the hill as guard. He searched the barren hills, but saw no sign of life. "Not even much vegetation," he mused to himself. In sight were a few low bushes, some kind of thistles, and a handful of cacti. In the distance, some green spots were apparent, marking oases.

As he scanned the desert hills, he felt pressure, like someone crying out for help. Aid he needed to supply. He felt it mount higher while images of Angelique and Drew filled his mind. He had no doubt this came from God. He wanted Dane to pray for them. He knelt and pleaded for the help he felt sure Angelique and Drew needed now. Dane wanted to fly to their rescue, but he couldn't. He didn't know where they were. Only the Lord could help them now. He begged with all of his might for God to meet their needs.

All the while he prayed, he also knew his men were depending on him to be their lookout and he didn't close his eyes, but kept them active.

Movement towards the north snagged his attention. At the same time the pressure left him. Whatever happened to them now remained in God's hands. He needed to concentrate on the here and now. He ducked for cover, and using the binoculars with care so they wouldn't reflect the sun, scanned the hills. A group of Arabs jumped into view, along with his heart. They were spread out in a line abreast, watching the ground, moving from the northwest towards the southeast. Dane saw one of them pull his camel to a stop and fling his arm up in the air. The others gathered around him, staring at the ground.

"Found our tracks," Dane muttered to himself, his mind now focused on the problem materializing in front of him. One of them looked up, straight at Dane, their eyes meeting through the binoculars. Dane froze. He knew not moving would keep him invisible to the Arab. He watched the man's face in the glasses, a sly, cruel looking man with grey appearing in his beard. The Arab broke the unseen eye contact, turned to his comrades and spoke unheard orders to them. They turned in the direction of the camp. Dane counted nine of them.

Dane eased through the rocks, being careful to keep under cover, until he looked down into the camp. He saw Tielson and tossed a rock to catch his attention. When Tielson looked up, Dane pointed in the direction the Arabs were coming and held up nine fingers. Tielson nodded his understanding. He alerted the others and they assumed their defensive positions. Dane melted away.

As the Arabs came into view, Bob Tielson picked out his target. Some sixth sense warned the Arab and he halted, looking around. Tielson squeezed the trigger. The Arab tumbled off his camel and lay still on the ground. Three more rifle shots rang out and another Arab fell to the ground. All the Arabs disappeared from sight as if ghosts. Tielson wiped his sweaty face and a bullet ricocheted off the rock he hid behind. He fired back and heard the whine of his bullet as it smashed off a rock. A few minutes later he saw a bush twitch and he sent a round through it. At once three bullets smashed into his rock, cutting his face with rock fragments. He heard Fredericks off to his right and then Zabronski above and behind him return fire.

High above them all, Dane lay hidden in the rocks, waiting and watching for an opportunity to whittle down the odds. Undetected by the attacking Arabs, his eyes roved over the terrain while his body waited motionless.

Webster caught a glimpse of a shadowy figure and fired, but in his haste shot too high. Rifle fire bracketed his position.

By now, the Arabs had pegged the positions of the four Americans and started working their way around them. Sporadic gunfire erupted whenever one side would catch a glimpse of the other. A bullet burned Fredericks' hand. Another nicked Webster's leg.

A single gunshot rang out. An Arab threw up his hands and slid down the slope. Startled, the Arab leader, Ali, looked around. Where did the shot come from? His desert wise eyes saw nothing, and yet there must be a fifth enemy somewhere. He felt a premonition it must be the Fox he mentioned two days ago. He motioned for his men to keep up the pressure while he kept an eye out for wherever the Fox hid.

Another half an hour passed, with an occasional burst of fire as he tightened the circle about the Americans. His divided attention cost him as Tielson saw him dodge from one rock to another. A bullet smashed into Ali's shoulder. The experienced bandit clamped his mouth shut, not uttering a sound from the pain.

Then another single shot spat again. An Arab howled in pain, grabbing his side. Ali reached out and pulled his companion to safety. The spreading red stain on the black robe revealed the extent of the injury.

Ali growled in mixed frustrated anger and worry. Three of his men were dead and another badly wounded. He himself nursed a flesh wound, and he still didn't know from where the hidden marksman fired. He scanned the slope above him, and his heart froze. If the Fox lay up there near the top, it would only be a matter of time before more of his men would be killed. Since no firing came from there at first, he assumed the hill empty of enemies. He'd allowed his men to come in too close and now they were in real danger from the infidel. Under his breath, he cursed the Fox for his cunning and then raised his voice, "Back, my children, back to the camels."

Zabronski, from his position above Tielson, realized the Arabs were pulling back. He watched one Arab trying to draw a bead on Tielson before leaving. The angle didn't allow for a clean shot. Zabronski aimed his rifle and squeezed the trigger. The rock exploded inches from Tielson's face. Startled, he jerked his head up. An Arab bullet found its mark. Tielson slumped down, dead.

After the Arabs' departure, Webster and Fredericks gathered around their fallen comrade while Dane watched to make sure the Arabs departed. He rose from his hiding place and sped down the slope to the gathering "What's wrong," he demanded.

Fredericks stood aside. "It's Tielson, he's dead."

"Oh no," Dane moaned, dropping to his knees. He checked for a pulse. Finding none, for a long moment he knelt with bowed head. Then with profound sorrow he gathered his friend's personal belongings together to take with him.

While Dane busied himself, Zabronski, with an innocent expression, pulled Fredericks aside. "See what I mean about people dying in battle? Are you with us or not?"

"You killed Tielson?" Fredericks asked, shock rocking him.

"Check the body, an Arab killed him," Zabronski smirked.

Fredericks looked at the big man and shivered. How could he accuse Zabronski of murdering Tielson without proof? Who would believe him? If Zabronski killed Tielson so easy, what chance did he, Fredericks, have? Feeling like an animal caught in a trap, and overawed by the big, wily man, Fredericks jerked a nod.

"Good man," Zabronski clapped him on the shoulder with a jovial laugh.

"What do you want me to do?" Fredericks

asked, shoulders slumping in misery.

"Nothing. Don't interfere, and you'll get a full share of the treasure."

Chapter Thirty

Dane returned to Tielson's body with real distress on his face. "We don't have anything to dig a grave with, and I don't want to leave him out here." He sighed. "Well, let's put it in the overhang for now." Zabronski volunteered to help. The two of them carried the body and placed it at the back of the overhang.

As the sun sank behind the mountains in the west, they heard a truck motor coming closer. Alarmed, Dane barked, "Hide, wait for me before shooting." He watched a German truck come into sight. He readied his weapon. Then it stopped out of range. Puzzled by its action, Dane stared, trying to get a glimpse of the figures in the cab. A woman climbed out, and Dane recognized Angelique. He stood up and waved. She returned the gesture and climbed back into the truck, which started up again. It came close enough for Dane to see the captain driving. Dane ran down the slope to greet them.

Zabronski stared at the truck and saw all of his plans go up in smoke. With the truck, there would be no need to backtrack to get the halftrack and loot. He knew full well the corporal and captain regarded it as unimportant and would not go after it.

He must come up with another idea and at once. While the other three conversed, Zabronski gathered his henchmen and hatched another plan.

"What happened?" panted Dane. Drew started to explain but Dane waved him off, "Did you get the information?"

"Yes, but what's the matter?" Drew asked, confused by Dane's demeanor.

"We were attacked by Arabs. We drove them off, but I'll bet anything they'll be back tonight. They killed Tielson."

"Oh, no," gasped Angelique.

Drew stared at Dane. "And I expect we're being trailed from town, to boot. We have to leave now." By then Zabronski and the others joined them. The captain ordered, "Break camp and load up the truck. We can't go back by Faid Pass. We'll have to go south around the mountains and back northwest to our lines."

Webster blinked at the change in the officer. Instead of asking questions and relying on Shaw, Matthews issued commands, taking control.

With a chorus of, "Yes, sirs,'" the soldiers scurried around.

Zabronski took careful stock of everyone's position. Shaw found an iron rod in the truck and was trying to cave in part of the overhang to bury

Tielson, Angelique put her belongings in the back of the truck and watched the corporal. The captain carried an armful of stuff towards the truck. Zabronski nodded to Webster and waited for Matthews at the back of the truck. "Hey Captain, did you see this?" Zabronski held back the flap and pointed to something in the bed of the truck.

"I haven't looked back there, what is it?" Drew tried to see what Zabronski indicted.

Zabronski lifted his rifle butt and brought it crashing down on the captain's head. He crumpled to the ground. Zabronski picked the body up and heaved it into the truck. He crawled in after it. After tying and gaging the unconscious man, he scrambled out again.

Webster wandered over to Angelique and touched her arm to get her attention. "Ma'am, the captain wants to see you at the back of the truck."

"Oh, *oui*," Angelique hurried over to see what Drew wanted while Webster moved over to Fredericks and whispered in his ear. The two of them walked to the truck. When Angelique reached the back of the truck, she didn't see anyone, so she lifted the flap to look into the bed. She felt something stick into her back, and a hand covered her mouth.

"Make any noise and it'll be your last,"

hissed Zabronski's voice in her ear. "Get in," he commanded.

She looked down and saw a knife in his hand. Obedient to the threat, she climbed into the back of the truck. He tied and gagged her and left her lying beside Drew. Holding the captain's pistol, he went back to the front of the truck. Webster climbed in the back and Fredericks got under the wheel and started the truck.

Dane jabbed the roof of the overhang. Again and again, he stabbed the rocky, stubborn soil, working out his grief of Tielson's death. Dirt trickled down. He plunged the iron rod with all his strength into the ceiling once more. The trickle became a torrent. Once, twice more and chunks began falling. He jumped back as a whole section collapsed, covering the body.

He wiped his hands as he heard the motor start. *They must be ready to go*, he thought as he picked up his submachine gun and got to his feet. He took a step and noticed something glittering on the ground by his feet. *A clip of ammo? What's it doing here?* He squatted down to pick it up.

The action saved his life.

Zabronski aimed and fired as Dane ducked down. The bullet, instead of striking him in the chest, hit his right shoulder and spilled him to the ground. He rolled, gun out, looking for his assailant. He saw Zabronski standing on the far side of the truck, a look of surprise on his face at having missed such an easy target, and holding a pistol pointed at Dane.

Shock at the identity of his assailant stunned Dane for a second. He squeezed the trigger of his gun and sprayed bullets, but missed as Zabronski jumped in the truck and hollered, "Go, go!"

Where are Angelique and the captain? Dane spared a quick look around but didn't see them. *They must be in the truck* He held his gun low and fired at the tires of the disappearing truck, trying not to hit anyone inside. He saw with satisfaction he hit one of the dual tires. It wasn't enough. The truck kept going.

After it disappeared into the distance, he sat there, surprised at the rapid turn of events, trying to grasp what happened. "First things first," he muttered and applied sulpha powder and a bandage to his shoulder, using his teeth to help tie it. As far as he could tell, it didn't appear to be a major wound. The bullet passed through the top of his shoulder, somehow missing the bones. Pain began as the shock wore off.

He took stock of his belongings. He possessed his submachine gun and spare ammo, a canteen almost full of water, a hand grenade which belonged to Tielson plus his own, giving him two. He had no food, and the nearest Americans were over fifty miles away as the crow flies. But he didn't have wings and would have to travel about twice as far. But the questions were, where was Zabronski taking the others, and why break away now?

Dane bowed his head. "Lord, you know what's going on and why. Where are they going? Is there a way I can rescue Drew and Angelique? Lord, I need you to direct my steps now, and I cannot afford to make a mistake. Lord, give me wisdom. I need you now, Drew needs you now, Angelique needs you now. Oh God, help me."

He sat there with his eyes closed, thinking. They'd been on the verge of heading south, and the halftrack and loot were north. He opened his eyes. *So that's why Zabronski fled at this time. He wants the loot. He doesn't know the chests and halftrack are hidden in different places. Drew will resist showing Zabronski where they are, knowing once he did, Zabronski would have no further use for him and kill him. But Zabronski also has Angelique, and could use her to force Drew to tell him.* With ruthless determination Dane forced from his mind the methods Zabronski would use. *If Drew resists long enough, and goes to the halftrack first, it might give me time to get to the hidden treasure before them. I also needed to get out of here. The Arabs are not far away and would have heard the gunfire.* He got to his feet, took his bearings, and trotted north, a set look to his face and a greenish cast to his eyes.

Chapter Thirty-One

Lindisl pounded his desk in fury. "Idiots! Imbeciles!" he shouted at the line of unfortunate soldiers, one of them shirtless. "How could you let one *dumkopff* American outsmart all of you and escape?" The German soldiers stood stiff as ramrods while Abu tried to become invisible. "I will deal with all of you when I return," he threatened. "Captain Heidelstrauss," he roared. When the captain ran in, Lindisl issued orders to him. "Make ready my *kubelwagon* and driver, and another *kubelwagon* and five soldiers who share half a brain between them. The dog will come too," pointing to Abu.

Within half an hour, they left the city. In the growing dusk, they drove to where the American dumped the driver. From there they followed the tracks of the truck. After a couple of miles, they came to a place where an overhang once existed, part of it now collapsed. They saw the tracks heading north. Lindisl scowled at the sight. Where could they be going in that direction? All the passes were in the secure hands of the Germans. He looked with suspicion at the fresh collapsed dirt. "See what's under there," he ordered.

While some of the men dug into the mound, Abu wandered around trying to make sense of the footprints. He found the camel tracks and wondered about them. Scouting around, he found a bloodstain on the ground. He realized a battle must have been fought here. He heard a shout from the digging men and turned around. In front of him were five Arabs. "Ali," Abu with a beaming expression greeted the leader.

"Abu, my brother," the leader welcomed the other with equal joy.

"Ali, do you know what happened here?" Abu asked.

Ali's face darkened as he recounted the events of the afternoon. "Why are you here, my brother?" Ali asked.

Abu explained his presence, and then went on. "There's money involved. The German leader has a halftrack loaded with treasure somewhere out here."

"Treasure?" The word caught Ali's attention. His agile mind put two and two together and he realized what must have happened. "Not any more, he doesn't," he answered his brother. "Those American's took it. We followed the trail to the road between Kairouan and Sfax and lost it." The two men's faces turned greedy. "What if we join forces with the German's until the money is found? Then we shall see which sly one keeps the treasure."

They heard Lindisl bellowing for Abu, and the group of Arabs walked out. They saw the disinterred American body with the Germans surrounding it.

"Who's this?" Lindisl demanded, pointing to the newcomers.

"This is my brother, Ali, *effendi.* The American dogs attacked them and killed some of his men. His blood is hot for revenge, and he is volunteering to help track them, *effendi.*"

"For a price, no doubt," Lindisl sneered.

"A very modest price," Ali bowed. "As he said, my blood is hot. Shall we say, a hundred francs?"

"Shall we say forty francs?" Lindisl smiled with a wolfish grin.

"Master, I am a poor man with mouths to feed. Ninety francs?"

Lindisl scowled. He hated this bartering which the Arabs loved to do. "Fifty."

"Master," Ali spread his hands. "They killed three of my children. Their wives and families need to be cared for. Eighty francs."

Lindisl drummed his fingers on the hood of

his *kubelwagon.* The tracking skills the Arabs possessed might be invaluable. "Sixty francs."

"I have a wounded brother. He will need much care. Seventy francs."

"Sixty-five, it's my final offer," Lindisl snapped.

Ali bowed. "It is agreed, Master."

The Arabs retrieved their camels and wounded comrade. The mixed force disappeared into the night.

Chapter Thirty-Two

After they traveled far enough to be safe from Dane, at least for a few minutes, Zabronski ordered Fredericks to stop the truck. He hopped out and walked to the back. Lifting the flap, he spotted Webster's shape. "Is the captain awake?"

Webster replied, "I think so, should I strike a light to see?"

"No, push him out."

As Webster pulled the bound figure of the captain out, Fredericks arrived. "What do you think you were doing back there?" his voice shook. "You didn't get him. He'll be coming after us now."

Zabronski glared at him. "Shut up. I said I'd shoot him and let him die."

"You didn't kill him, you wounded him. I tell you, he'll be coming after us. We've got to keep going."

"Shut up!" Zabronski roared as he raised his arm to strike Fredericks. "He doesn't have anything which can catch us." Zabronski wouldn't admit it, but he didn't want to remain here for long in case the corporal did follow them. He felt a cold shudder of what would happen if Shaw did catch up with them.

Fredericks subsided, but his mutters proved his unhappiness about the event.

Drew and Angelique's hearts rose; Dane was alive. Hurt, but now a chance of rescue existed.

Zabronski stood Drew up on his feet and removed his gag.

Drew wet his lips. "I'm in charge here," he commanded. "I order you two men to cover Zabronski and free us."

"No, I'm in charge," Zabronski sneered, "and you'll do what I say." He looked at his two followers. Webster grinned, thinking of all the money. Fredericks looked miserable, but did nothing. Satisfied, Zabronski turned back to the captain. "I say you'll tell us where you hid the halftrack."

"Halftrack?" Drew felt muddled. They had the truck, why want the halftrack too? "Why do you want…?" Illumination burst upon him like a high powered lamp. Zabronski wasn't after the halftrack, he wanted the loot. And he didn't know they were hidden in different places. The whole plan unfolded in Drew's mind, a plan which couldn't have been devised by any mere human. Not by him, not by Dane, not even by the diabolical Major Lindisl. It must have come from Someone greater than they, Someone all-powerful and all-knowing. Drew felt his blood chill as he realized the awesomeness of what happened. This is why they abandoned the halftrack. This is why it seemed like a good idea to hide the treasure in a separate place. If they'd kept the halftrack with the loot at the camp, then he would not have been hit on the head. He would have had a bullet in it. He went cold at the next thought. Then Angelique would have been at Zabronski's mercy.

His mind raced. If Dane wasn't shot too bad, if he would think of it, then he might head for where they'd buried the cases. If he, Drew, could delay Zabronski and the others, then maybe hope remained for Angelique and himself. He knew once Zabronski possessed the money, he would have no further use for the captain. Drew stood up as straight as he could and squared his jaw. "I am giving you a direct order. Place Zabronski under arrest and free myself and Miss DuBois," he ordered Webster and Fredericks.

They didn't respond any better than the last time.

Zabronski glared at the captain. He didn't have time to play games. The Arabs were around somewhere. Despite his bravado, he did not want to face Shaw again, wounded or not. "Tell me, where did you hide the halftrack?" he ordered right back.

"No." Drew braced himself for physical retaliation.

Instead, Zabronski gave a mysterious smile. "Pull Miss Dubois out," he said in a mild tone. As Webster helped slide her out of the truck, her skirt got caught up around her waist. Zabronski reached out and pulled it down. As he did so, he ran his hands down her legs. She shivered and tried to arch away. Drew bit his tongue to keep from saying something which would escalate the situation.

Zabronski leered at her, and then told Webster, "Bring her up to the front of the truck." The big man picked up Drew with ease, carried him to the passenger side of the cab and thrust him inside. With his hands tied behind his back and his legs bound, Drew squirmed around to find a more comfortable position.

Zabronski turned to his two henchmen, "Get in the back of the truck."

"What are you going to do?" Fredericks asked, nervous glances bouncing between Angelique and Zabronski.

"I'm going to find out where the halftrack is," he glared at Fredericks. "Now get in the back of the truck."

Fredericks looked at Angelique one last time before obeying Webster's tug on the arm and following him into the truck. Zabronski bent down and untied her legs. Using this rope, he tied one end to her hands which were bound behind her back. He fastened the other end to the headlight on the truck. Drew watched the proceedings through the windshield with mounting dread.

Zabronski leaned in the open side window. He asked Drew, "Now will you tell me where the halftrack is?" Drew shook his head. Zabronski shrugged, got in behind the wheel and started driving. As he went down the slope, he went slow enough so Angelique kept up by jogging. When he drove up the next slope she dropped to a walk. On the next slope down he sped up, forcing her to run. He drove faster, pulling off of her feet and dragging her.

"Stop," Drew yelled.

Zabronski gave an evil grin and said, "I can't hear you. Are you telling me the location of the halftrack?"

Drew shouted "Yes." He slumped when Zabronski stopped the truck.

"Where is it?" he demanded.

"It's in a draw about a quarter mile east of the Kairouan-Sfax highway."

"East of the highway?" Zabronski's mouth dropped open with amazement. "You stashed it so far away?"

Drew gave a defeated nod. Zabronski got out, untied Angelique from the truck, and shoved her into the front seat between him and Drew. She whimpered in pain behind her gag, and Drew saw one leg scratched and bloody. For the first time in his life he felt hatred for another man. He glared at Zabronski, wishing for just one chance to kill him.

Zabronski drove north until they saw headlights on the Faid-Sfax highway. He waited for a break in the traffic and continued north, driving up and down ridges. Drew braced his feet with his back to the door, hoping it wouldn't fly open. Angelique bounced around, with occasional moans, until she too braced her feet with her shoulder wedged behind Drew's shoulder. Drew whispered to her in French, "Be brave, *chéri.*"

After a while, Zabronski slowed to a stop. "Is this the draw you drove on?" he asked.

Drew looked around. "I don't know, everything looks different at night."

Zabronski cursed. "I think we've come far enough north, let's try it." He drove straight east until they came close to the highway. Ahead of them the road went over the draw on a low bridge, too small for a vehicle to pass under. Zabronski cursed again. He backed up until out of sight of the road. Seeing a drivable slope, he gunned the motor and climbed to the top instead of driving in reverse all the way back to the entrance. They bumped their way northwest until they intersected their route, then turned north until they reached the next draw. With a sinking heart, Drew recognized this as the turnoff.

"Is this the one?" Zabronski asked.

Drew tried to stall for time. "I'm not sure, it doesn't look right somehow."

Zabronski grabbed Angelique and said, "Let's go for another walk."

"Wait," Drew exclaimed. He took another look and gave a weary nod. "It's the right one."

Zabronski sneered and released her. He drove until they reached the highway, then sped across the empty road.

As the truck bounced along, Drew hoped no one would see the halftrack behind its covering. He breathed a sigh of relief when Zabronski drove past it. *I have to give Dane every possible moment to reach us. But what if he isn't coming?* The fear chilled Drew to the bone. *I have to believe he's on the way. He's our only hope.*

The route they traveled on came to an abrupt halt a few minutes later. A rock blocked the path. Zabronski slammed on the brakes. Enraged, he shouted at Drew. 'You lied to me. Where is it? I'll break every bone in your body if you don't tell."

Drew pretended to be dumb. He looked around with a puzzled look. "You must have driven past it. I know this is the right draw."

"We didn't pass any halftrack," Zabronski roared, pounding the steering wheel.

Drew turned innocent eyes towards his captor. "We covered it up with brush."

"What?" Zabronski opened and closed his mouth. Then fury convulsed his face, such anger Drew never saw before in any person.

Zabronski smashed his fist into Angelique's face with such force her head banged on the rear window. "That's for not telling me sooner," he ground out from between his teeth. He yanked the truck in reverse and began backing up.

Hatred boiled in Drew's heart as he glared at the Russian, emotion which Drew clamped down on. He must use his brain and not his brawn if they were to have any chance of escape.

Chapter Thirty-Three

When Zabronski saw some bushes piled at the side of the gully he stopped. "Is this it?" he growled.

"Yes," Drew admitted with an inward sigh.

Zabronski shut off the motor and the three renegades jumped out. They ran over and pulled the bushes out of the way, exposing the front end of the vehicle. Because of how Dane jammed the vehicle in, they couldn't see the cargo area. Zabronski got in, and after two tries got the halftrack out of the hole it was wedged into. Then the three of them dove into the back of the halftrack.

Drew looked at Angelique, her face white and strained, a bruise forming on the side of her head. "Courage my dear, we have to give Dane enough time to get to the cases." Her eyes asked the question her gagged mouth couldn't. "We hid the cases in a different location than the halftrack."

She closed her eyes and sagged in relief, knowing they weren't about to be killed in the next few minutes. She knew, or thought she knew, as soon as Zabronski possessed the treasure she and Drew would die.

Drew heard angry exclamations from his

three captors. They charged from the halftrack back to the truck. Zabronski wrenched open the door and dragged Drew out. "Where are they?" he shouted as he shook the bound man like a rag doll.

"It's right there," Drew managed to get out. "You were just in it."

"Not the halftrack, the cases that were in it," Zabronski roared.

Drew looked innocent. "You never asked about them, only the halftrack."

Zabronski balled his fist and smashed the other man in the mouth. Unable to break his fall, Drew somersaulted, his face hitting the ground. He tasted blood in his mouth, his ears rang, and gravel bit into his face. He knew another blow would knock him out, and he tried to think of something to say to provoke another hit.

"You think you're a big man," he taunted his captor. "Shaw outsmarted you, he whipped you in a fistfight, and when you shot and wounded him, you ran like a scared rabbit.

Enraged, Zabronski yanked Drew to his feet and reared back to hit him again.

Anything to cause delay, Drew thought as he braced himself as best he could.

Webster grabbed Zabronski's arm with both hands. "Wait, we'll never find the money if you kill him."

For a moment rage battled for reason within the Russian. At last he dropped his arm and shook Webster off. He glared at the captain. "Where's the money?"

Drew stared back, mouth clamped shut.

Zabronski stomped to the truck and dragged Angelique out of the cab. He yanked down her gag, and before she could move, fastened his lips on hers. As she tried to pull her head away, he shifted his hold freeing up a hand, which disappeared under her clothing. She redoubled her efforts to writhe away, with as little success.

Drew heard her moans. He couldn't stand it anymore and yelled, "That's enough, I'll tell." Still Zabronski ground on and more of her skin appeared. "If you don't stop right now, I'll never tell you," Drew thundered at his captor.

After a few more seconds Zabronski lifted his head. He leered at Angelique while he said to Drew, "You give up too easy." He shot a fierce look at Drew while keeping his hold on the girl. "Where is it?"

"On down this gully," Drew answered as he sagged in defeat.

Zabronski weighed his options, hoisted the girl into his arms, and commanded the other two men, "Put him into the cab of the halftrack."

"Why the halftrack, why not stay with the truck?" asked Webster.

"Because the halftrack is better for cross country travel, the truck is low on gas, and has a flat tire," Zabronski snapped. When he reached the halftrack, he tossed Angelique into the cab and got in behind the wheel. Webster and Fredericks helped the captain in beside Angelique and then they climbed into the back of the vehicle.

Drew and Angelique braced themselves like they did in the truck. Angelique wiped her mouth on Drew's shirt sleeve as vigorous as she could.

As Drew braced himself, he wondered if he'd bought Dane enough time to reach the hidden loot. *If he's coming.* As he thought of Dane, Drew thought of what Dane told them from the Bible. He stiffened as realization hit him. It felt like scales dropped from his eyes. He understood what Dane said about salvation. HE UNDERSTOOD! Just like he, Drew, was helpless to save himself and totally relying on someone else to rescue him, so he could not save himself from his sins. He had to totally and completely rely on Jesus Christ and His sacrifice on the cross to save him from the consequences of sin. Drew bowed his head, and in the bouncing vehicle with Angelique staring at him in amazement, he prayed. "Jesus, I understand I'm a sinner, I know there is nothing I can do of my own self to wipe away my sins. I know you paid for my sins on the cross, and I accept your sacrifice. I ask you to forgive my sins and come into my heart."

When Drew raised his head, he'd become a new creature. A new emotion filled him. Freed for the first time in his life of the burden of sin, a load he didn't realize he carried until he met Dane and heard the Word of God. He felt the presence of the Holy Spirit in his heart, just like Dane described. He knew within an hour he could be dead, but he felt no panic because he knew he would be with Jesus.

He turned his head towards Angelique with a look of wonder, "Angelique, I understand what Dane told us. I just now accepted Jesus as my savior, and it's like what Dane described. I'm free from sin; I feel Jesus in my heart."

Before Angelique could answer, Zabronski roared, "Shaddup. I don't want to hear anything about Jesus. I've heard enough sermonizing."

Drew subsided and Zabronski drove to the road. Seeing it empty of traffic, he clanked across and continued on in the draw. Once out of sight of the highway, Zabronski pulled to a stop. He glared at Drew. "You tell me when we reach the cases at once or I'll have some fun with the girlie," he threatened.

"Yes," Drew sighed. He'd hoped to engineer another delay.

They drove to where the cases were hidden. "Here they are," Drew announced and Zabronski stopped the vehicle. As the three American's jumped out, Zabronski held up his hand for quiet. In the distance they heard the sound of vehicles.

"Germans," shouted Fredericks, and started to jump back in.

"No," Zabronski stopped him, "The cases first. Where are they?" he demanded from Drew.

"There," he pointed with his chin. Zabronski growled, yanked Drew from the cab and cut his bonds. "Show me where," Zabronski demanded again.

Drew stumbled over to where they were hidden, "Here." As the blood returned to his feet and hands, it caused excruciating pain, but he tried to hide it from his captors.

Zabronski pushed him to the ground. "Dig them out." As Drew started to unearth the first case, gritting his teeth against the pain, Webster and Fredericks began digging up the other two. Zabronski kept watch for approaching enemies.

"Fredericks, you and the captain take the first one, Webster and I will take the second.

Hurry," he commanded when the cases were uncovered. Drew and Fredericks grabbed the first case, carried it over to the halftrack and shoved it in. Zabronski and Webster pushed their case in while the other two went back for the third case. They picked it up and started walking towards the vehicle. Drew prayed in his heart. *Lord, this is it. Please protect us. Angelique isn't saved yet, please give her the chance. God, where is Dane? Help him if you can.*

In the cab Angelique sobbed, remembering how the awful man kissed her. She still tasted him on her lips. She tried to scrub them on her shoulder, but moving it caused such pain. And where he put his hand made her shudder at the remembrance of his touch. *Mon Dieu*, what did he plan for her now he'd taken the treasure? Earlier the threat of death filled her with fear. Now terror of him keeping her alive drowned out everything else. She broke down, crying with a broken heart. In her despair, she turned to the one possible help still available to her: Dane and his God. She started praying, "God, if you are real, if what Dane and Drew said to me is true, then save us. If you prove to me you exist, then I'll believe in You."

Chapter Thirty-Four

The German-Arab force followed the truck tracks from the camp at the overhang. Two Arabs went in front on foot. Even though a moonless night, the desert-wise trackers followed the trail of the truck at a trot. The *kubelwagons* followed them, while Ali and his remaining Arabs on camelback trailed behind. They came to the place where the truck turned east towards the low bridge. They traveled down the draw towards the bridge, then followed the tracks over the ridge to the next draw. They missed the Americans as they drove past on the way to the cases, which everyone without knowing it passed by the turnoff earlier.

The two Arabs in front stopped and searched the ground for tracks in the next draw. With great excitement they called out and pointed to the ground. Abu got out of the *kubelwagon* and hurried over to them.

"What is it?" demanded Lindisl who followed Abu.

"*Effendi,* the truck turned and went northeast, but a halftrack came from the northeast and went west up this draw a few minutes ago. Listen," he held up his hand. They heard the faint

265

sound of the halftrack in the clear desert air. Then they couldn't hear it anymore. All of them looked at each other.

"They stopped," Ali said and Abu translated.

"Let's go," ordered Lindisl. They hurried back to their vehicles and camels. Mounting up, they headed in the direction of the sound.

After a few minutes one of the lead Arabs stopped and waited for the major's *kubelwagon* to catch up. He said something to Abu, who turned to Lindisl. "*Effendi,* stop the vehicles and turn off the engines." Lindisl gave the order and quiet descended over the desert once more. "*Effendi*, they are still stopped and they are close. They will hear the engines if we continue. If we hurry on foot we can surprise them."

Lindisl considered the advice and then issued orders. "You two," pointing to the two German drivers, "remain with the *kubelwagons*, and the wounded Arab with the camels. The rest of us will continue on foot. When you hear firing, come at once." Lindisl pointed to the two trackers and motioned for them to lead off. Then he waved the remainder on and they started moving on up the draw. Lindisl's heart beat faster. *The halftrack must have the loot on it. At last I have my property back.*

Ali fixated on the Fox. *Soon I'll be face to*

face with the infidel who killed my men.

Treasure danced in Abu's mind. *How can we take it from cursed Major Lindisl?*

***

Since leaving the camp, Dane followed the North Star towards where the treasure cases were hidden. The moonless night made details of the terrain ahead of him hard to make out. He kept up his mile-eating trot as much as he could, dropping to a walk when climbing up ridges. Each slow down filled him with anxiety. Shoving aside the pain from his shoulder, he concentrated on the goal of reaching the loot before Zabronski.

As he ran, he prayed. *Lord, please keep Angelique and Drew safe. Please direct me to the right place at the right time. Dear God, I don't know what Zabronski's intentions are, but they can't be good. Only You can help them now in their hour of need. God, please don't let them die before they've accepted You as their savior. God, please save them.*

At last he reached a place where he knew the hidden cases must be close by. He stopped at the top of a ridge. Which direction did they lay? Over the sound of his panting, Dane heard the faint, approaching sound of an engine. *It must be them*, he thought. *It sounds like it's a rise or two away.*

267

He took off running down the slope. As he raced across a level area, the ground disappeared in front of him. What he thought a dark colored patch of earth turned out to be a narrow ravine. Going too fast to stop and the rift being too wide to jump, he took the one choice left to him.

He ran down the side of the ravine, his feet nimble as a mountain goat, barely touching the ground before springing for the next step, his heart in his mouth. He knew one misstep would send him tumbling head over heels. Under the present circumstances, a broken neck or leg, either one, would mean his death, a long, lingering one. His feet smacked into the bottom of the ravine. The momentum almost drove him to his knees. He sprang up the other side, hands and feet clawing for holds. Once both feet slipped and he caught himself with his right hand. The pain in his shoulder tore at him. He forced himself on.

He reached the top and heaved himself over, the blood drumming in his ears, gasping for breath, shocked he'd made it out without injury. As he breathed a prayer of thankfulness, his ears stopped drumming and he heard silence, or almost. He sat up. "They've stopped. They must be at the cache," he told himself. Were his ears still drumming? Then he realized he heard more vehicles. He got up and started running towards the next rise, being more careful this time.

As he climbed the ridge, the motor sounds stopped. He crept to the top of the ridge and looked down. Below and to his left he made out the bulk of the halftrack. Two men were carrying a case towards the vehicle. As Dane tried to make out who the two men were, movement caught the corner of his eye. He froze and tried to see what caused it. Then he caught a gleam of metal. By straining his eyes he made out a form of someone. A black-robed figure pointed a long rifle towards the two men with the case.

Before he could move, the Arab shot. One of the two men stumbled and fell. Gunfire erupted from down the draw. Dane spotted the group of enemies shooting towards the halftrack. The other figure with the case fell to the ground.

Lindisl felt elation sweep over him, he had them. "Attack," he screamed and led his men in a charge around the shoulder of the draw.

Dane yanked out a grenade, pulled the pin and threw it. It exploded right in front of the Germans, knocking one of them to the ground. Guns started firing from the back of the halftrack. More Germans went down. Dane snatched up his submachine gun and shot the Arab who'd fired first.

269

A bullet struck next to his head, peppering him with rock fragments. He ducked and rolled. Spotting where the bullet came from, he fired at the Arab who managed to duck behind a rock.

Dane heard the roar of approaching vehicles, and leaving the fight, moved back down the ridge and to his right to intercept them. He popped his head over the top of the ridge, and waited for them to appear. When two *kubelwagons* came into range, he heaved his last grenade. The first *kubelwagon* exploded and blocked the path. He shot at the second *kubelwagon* and saw the driver bail out. Dane melted away into the darkness, hurrying to get back to the halftrack.

***

Lindisl couldn't believe what happened. One minute his men were sweeping onward to victory, the enemy soldiers falling, and then came an explosion which knocked him down. He saw his men collapsing and dying. He watched an Arab fall. Lindisl jumped to his feet and ran back towards the advancing *kubelwagons.* One exploded ten feet in front of him. A barrage of bullets hit the second one, then the firing stopped. He stood in stunned surprise as Abu and Ali ran by him. He met them by the second *kubelwagon* as his driver crawled out of hiding and joined them. They heard a few more

270

shots from the battle behind them. Lindisl jumped at the sound of the halftrack starting up and driving away.

"After them," he yelled. He spun around and stopped, staring at a flattened tire on the *kubelwagon.* He slumped as the realization of his defeat hit him.

Ali shook with a mixture of fury and fear. "That cursed infidel American Fox. He trapped us again. Now more of my men are gone, and for what, my brother? All I have is an empty purse and more empty camels. I must have revenge and I must have the treasure to rebuild with."

Abu soothed him. "We will, my brother, we will." They spoke in their native Derja, which Major Lindisl did not understand, nor any of his men. As they spoke, two more Arabs materialized out of the darkness.

In shock, Lindisl staggered forward. "What happened, what went wrong?" he asked Abu. "We had them, they were being destroyed."

"My brother claims it is an American Fox. He has defeated and outwitted Ali several times already. We must get him."

"We will, we will," Lindisl grunted back, his mind in turmoil over the unbelievable turn of events in the last few minutes. He shook himself and

271

regained his composure. "I need reinforcements. I'll call for more men and a halftrack to rendezvous with us. In the morning I'll order planes to comb the desert for them," he said out loud. He looked at his watch. It seemed incredible, but the hands pointed to midnight. *So much has happened in so little time.*

He stood with his hands on his hips, pondering the next move. Where would those Americans go? Not northward, Von Arnim's army lay there. German troops controlled Faid Pass to the west. Rommel's army was advancing from the south. Southwest. Lindisl snapped his fingers. Their one escape route lay in the gap between the two German armies who hadn't linked up yet.

He stomped over to the surviving *kubelwagon* and eyeballed the shot up vehicle. "Does this still run and does the radio work?" he asked the driver.

After a quick check, he answered, "*Jawohl* to both, *Herr* Major."

"Good," Lindisl grunted. 'Now change the tire." While the driver worked and Arabs patched up the wounded, Lindisl radioed up Captain Heidelstrauss. "Captain, order a squad of soldiers in a halftrack to leave at once and meet up with me. Right now I'm northwest of Sfax and will be traveling southwest. Call the airfield and have planes search the desert at first light for a German halftrack. Don't attack unless they're positive it's not being driven by Germans. I'm on the trail of an American the Arabs called The Fox. Also alert the local commander at Faid Pass about the possibility of a German halftrack being driven by Americans and a French woman trying to sneak through."

Heidelstrauss stuttered for a moment then answered, "*Jawohl, Herr* Major."

Lindisl broke the connection and muttered, "That should cover all the possibilities."

Chapter Thirty-Five

As Drew helped carry the last case, a shot rang out. White-hot pain seared his leg which toppled him to the ground. He grabbed hold to shut off the torment as well as the flow of blood staining his pants leg. A burst of firing felled Fredericks. He watched through agonized eyes as German soldiers ran towards him. An explosion tore into the group. Germans flew through the air. A submachine gun opened up from the ridge.

It's Dane, he made it in the nick of time. Drew felt like cheering.

Zabronski and Webster opened up from behind the halftrack. More Germans fell.

Angelique cowered in the cab of the halftrack, sobbing in mingled fear, joy and pain. They were being rescued. But all the shooting and explosions scared her, and her shoulder and leg were hurting.

Drew dragged himself to behind the case and hid. He listened to Fredericks' groans of pain. As the firing died down, he heard Fredericks cry out, "Mother, Mother," and then "Mandie." Then he went silent.

I wonder who Mandie is? Drew thought.

Then another shot rang out, and he saw Webster fall. Zabronski fired twice and silence fell again.

Zabronski peered out from behind the half-track. He saw the third case out there and realized it's the one containing the bags of money. He must have it. Using the utmost caution, he poked his head out and looked all around. Moans of the wounded broke the quiet. Making a decision, he raced to the case. He bent low, grabbed one end and ran back to the halftrack, the other end of the case bouncing along behind him. He laid his rifle in the bed of the halftrack and heaved the case into the vehicle. *I did it. I have the money and the girl and nobody to share with. I can get in the vehicle and drive off. I did it,* he exalted to himself.

"Zabronski," came the quiet voice from behind him.

Zabronski froze. The voice he hated. Not moving his body, he turned his head, searching the shadows. "How did you get here," he asked, trying to pinpoint Shaw's location.

"I walked. Now turn around and hold your hands up," Dane commanded.

Zabronski peered into the dark. There, it looked like a shadow beside a rock. His hand closed on his gun. "There's more than enough here for the two of us," he suggested, and then paused.

Silence.

Yanking his rifle out, he twisted and fired. *I got him.* A gun blazed back at him, BUT NOT FROM THE SHADOW! He felt the shock of bullets. The ground reached up and hit him. He stared at it, wondering where it came from. He felt strange. A deeper darkness than the night settled over his eyes. He shuddered and died. He opened his eyes and felt the fires of hell burning him and started screaming, screams which lasted for all eternity.

Dane appeared from the other side of the rock. "Drew, Captain," he spoke with a loud whisper. He waited with bated breath, hoping against hope for an answer.

"Here." A mound on the ground moved.

Dane crept towards Zabronski, alert for any movement from him or anywhere else in the area. Dane felt for a pulse and discovered none. He ran to Drew and dropped down beside him. "Are you hurt?"

"Yes, my leg," Drew groaned.

Dane made out the spreading dark patch on the pants. He whipped out his handkerchief and knotted it above the wound, making it a tourniquet. "Where's Angelique?"

"In the cab," Drew panted.

276

"We have to leave before they come back", Dane pointed out. Using his left arm, he heaved Drew to his feet and they stumbled to the halftrack. Propping Drew against the side of the vehicle, Dane jerked open the door. Angelique's white tear-stained face stared back at him.

"Angelique, are you hurt?" He saw her hands were tied behind her. He pulled out his knife and cut her bonds. Her arms dropped to her sides, lifeless from the abuse they'd taken.

"Oh Dane, Dane." She threw herself into his arms, crying from relief and pain from the returning circulation.

He held her close to him, feeling her shudders. He looked into her dear face. "Are you hurt?" he asked again.

"*Oui*, my shoulder and leg. Oh Dane, you came, you came. I prayed and prayed, and you came." She stared crying again.

Dane gave her a gentle shake. "We aren't free yet. I'll be right back." He ran to check on Fredericks and Webster. Finding both dead, he grabbed their rifles, ammunition and canteens. Then he raced to Zabronski's body and gathered up his rifle, ammo, canteen and grenade.

He ran back to the halftrack and tossed everything into the back of the vehicle. By then

Drew had climbed in. Dane jumped into the cab, and took off.

As soon as he could, he got out of the draw and headed southwest. About twenty minutes later, he pulled to a stop and everyone started babbling at the same time.

"Where did you come from?"

"What happened to you?"

"How bad are you hurt?"

The three of them stopped talking, looked at each other and burst out in almost hysterical laughter, trying to put their arms around each other.

Dane regained his composure first. "We have to release the tourniquet."

Drew nodded and loosened it. He spoke with a thoughtful frown. "We have about a hundred miles to go to reach friendly lines, going cross country like we have to. I don't think we're going to make it by sun up."

Dane tapped the fuel gauge. "And I don't think we have enough fuel either, but it'll be close." He winced at the pain in his shoulder from the movement.

Angelique noticed. "Are you hurt bad, *mon chéri?*"

"He got me in the shoulder," Dane replied as he put the vehicle in gear. "Better tighten up the tourniquet."

Drew complied as Angelique drew a deep breath to make her announcement. "*Mes chéris,* I prayed to God that if he saved us, then I would serve him."

"No," both men shouted in unison.

As Dane looked at Drew in surprise, Drew tried to explain in halting words what he knew. "You have to admit you are a sinner and, and you can do nothing of, or by, yourself to warrant God's forgiveness of your sins. Only by believing in Jesus Christ can your sins be forgiven. Then you can serve God, like I did tonight."

Dane looked over at him with an incredulous expression. "You got saved tonight?"

"Yes," Drew averred with a firm nod.

"Praise God, praise God, praise God," Dane hammered the steering wheel in joy. Then he turned to Angelique, "If you try to serve God without surrendering to Jesus, then you'll be serving him in your own strength and you'll fail. But if you accept Jesus as your savior first, then you'll serve Him with God's strength and you'll succeed."

Angelique looked at him. "I believe Jesus died for my sins, and I want him to save me. Will you show me how?"

"Just pray and tell God what you told me.

I'll pray first and you pray after me. Dear Lord, Angelique knows she's a sinner, she cannot save herself, and only Jesus can save her. Please forgive her sins, wipe them away with the blood of Jesus Christ, and come and enter her heart. Amen."

Angelique closed her eyes and bowed her head, "*Mon Dieu*, I have sinned. I cannot wash away my sins, only the blood shed by Jesus can do that. I ask you to forgive me, and enter my heart. Amen." Angelique lifted her head with the same wonder Drew felt before. "I understand," she breathed. "I understand." She looked into the face of Dane, sitting next to her, and saw joy and happiness, and something else. She saw he loved her.

Dane beamed at her, his heart in his eyes. Not only had she accepted Jesus as her savior, but also he was now free to love her, to marry her. He couldn't ask her here and now, as they weren't alone and they were in great danger. He was willing to die to keep her safe, but, *Oh Lord, I don't want to die, not now,* he prayed. He would wait until they were safe before proposing. He hadn't been this happy since…since… well, he couldn't remember since when. He beamed again and then turned his mind to practical matters, like driving.

As they traveled, the three rejoiced together

in their newfound happiness in Christ. They knew, whatever happened in the future, they would always have this bond between them. They were brothers and sister in Christ first and foremost, and the bonds of deep friendship were forged this night.

After about another twenty minutes Dane pulled to a stop. "It's time to loosen the tourniquet again. Let's take a look at it."

Drew loosened the handkerchief but grumbled, "We can't be stopping every twenty minutes. We'll never get back."

Dane agreed, "We'll get the wounds bandaged up now and then drive all night long. We can't afford to lose any more time than we need to." He examined Drew's leg and saw the bullet had passed through the thigh muscle. Dane applied sulpha powder and bandages, then turned to Angelique. When he touched her shoulder she winced. "Try to move your arm," he commanded.

"I can't," she whimpered. Dane felt her shoulder and looked at both of his companions. "I think her shoulder is dislocated. How did it happen?"

Drew described how Zabronski dragged her.

Angelique shuddered at the look which came over Dane's face and the green flecks which burned in his eyes.

"Here," Drew said, "I know how to pop it back into place." He bent her elbow to 90 degrees and then rotated her arm and shoulder inward towards her chest. Then he balled one fist and put it in her armpit while rotating her arm and shoulder outward. She stiffened with pain but then it popped into place.

"Ooh, it feels so much better. Thank you, *mon chéri.*"

The two men examined her leg, and stared at each other, grim-faced. It was scraped, bloody and with gravel embedded in it. When she tried to bend it, she moaned in pain. "Angelique, honey," Drew explained, "This needs cleaned out. We can't do it here and now. Can you endure it until we reach a hospital in the morning?"

"*Oui,*" she nodded with a determined set of her jaw.

The two men looked at each other over her head. "Whatever happens," Drew said and Dane nodded. The two men sealed their vow in unspoken agreement. Whatever happened, they would make sure she would reach safety. Whatever it cost them.

They took off again, and as they traveled, they exchanged stories of what happened to them since Zabronski's attack.

As the night wore on, the three Christians

282

talked for a while, and then Angelique started dozing with her head on Drew's shoulder. As he looked at her, he realized he loved her, but he didn't know her feelings about him. Sometimes he thought she favored him, other times she looked to Dane. As he thought about it, he started to pray within himself, "Lord, whichever one of us is Your will for Angelique to marry, let the other accept it. Let there be no hard feelings to mar the fellowship and friendship we have now." A thought came into his mind. "And if she chooses neither of us, let us both accept it. Lord, whatever is best for Angelique, let it be done. In Jesus name I pray, Amen." He felt at peace, and furthermore if she did choose Dane, he could rejoice for them. He marveled at how Jesus had changed him already.

Chapter Thirty-Six

Captain Heidelstrauss hung up from talking to Major Lindisl and looked at the clock. Midnight. Didn't Lindisl ever sleep? Yes, of course he did, Heidelstrauss corrected himself. The major did, but he didn't expect his underlings to. Heidelstrauss let out his frustration in a monologue. "Now I'm expected to send out a patrol to rendezvous with him in the middle of the desert. If connections are missed, I know whose head will roll." He shuddered. "I hope it's figurative and not literal. And what's this about hunting some American Fox?" Puzzled, Heidelstrauss sighed and got on with the problem.

He placed a call to the barracks and talked to the officer on duty. "Lieutenant, Major Lindisl orders a squad in a halftrack to meet him out in the desert. Have the men take three days rations and plenty of extra fuel."

The mere mention of Major Lindisl's name silenced any protestations the lieutenant may have thought of making. Heidelstrauss decided to use some psychology, "Major Lindisl is tracking down some American calling himself The Fox."

"What?" the lieutenant sputtered. "Field

284

Marshal Rommel is The Fox. How dare some American take the name. The squad will be ready in ten minutes."

Heidelstrauss chuckled as he hung up, and then grew serious as he pulled out the map and pondered. Major Lindisl was northwest of Sfax and the fugitives were heading southwest. If the halftrack traveled straight west out of Sfax, they could meet up with Major Lindisl in a shorter amount of time than if they followed the direction of the enemy.

***

Out in the desert, Lindisl checked his resources. Three Germans were dead and two badly wounded. There remained himself, his driver and one *kubelwagon*. Of the Arabs, Abu and one other were unhurt. Ali and two Arabs were wounded but still able to continue, and one was able to ride but not fight. Lindisl gave his orders to Abu in French, "Your wounded man will take my two wounded men back to Sfax on camels. We will continue on and rendezvous with the halftrack. We will follow them and catch them. Let's go."

Abu passed on his orders to Ali. The two brothers exchanged knowing looks before Abu got in the *kubelwagon*. Ali gave his orders to his men. They mounted up and followed the vehicle. After everyone else departed, the remaining Arab slit the throats of the two Germans, stripped the bodies, and melted into the darkness with the three camels.

When Lindisl reached the road to Faid, he stopped and called Captain Heidelstrauss. "Where's the halftrack?" he asked.

"They're leaving town now," Heidelstrauss responded, and gave the frequency and call sign of the reinforcements. He also told the direction they would travel.

Lindisl conferred with Ali and Abu, "How far are we from Sfax?"

They looked at each other and shrugged, "About ten kilometers, *effendi*."

Lindisl called up the halftrack. "This is Major Lindisl. How far are you from Sfax?"

"Two or three kilometers, *Herr* Major."

Lindisl pondered for a moment. "We're about ten kilometers from Sfax traveling southwest. Keep motoring west until you are ten kilometers from town. Call when you reach there."

"*Jawohl, Herr* Major."

Lindisl ordered Ali, "Have your man follow their tracks. We will be right behind him."

***

As Sergeant Richter bounced along in the halftrack, he grumbled to the driver, "Why did it have to be me the lieutenant assigned to Lindisl."

His companion glanced at him. "What's the matter?"

Richter ground his teeth. "Because if you make any mistakes around the good major, he will make you pay. Take my advice and stay as far away from him as you can. And besides, today's my birthday. I've got a bottle of schnapps I'm planning on celebrating with tonight."

"There's plenty of time before then. We'll be back soon."

Richter brightened up. "Yeah, you're right." He smacked his lips. "I can almost taste it." A bottle Richter never got the chance to open.

The driver looked at the odometer. "We've gone ten kilometers."

Richter ordered, "Stop the vehicle." He climbed out and told the radio operator in the rear, "Call Major Lindisl and tell him we reached the appointed place."

"Can you hear our vehicle?" Lindisl demanded.

Richter listened to the silence of the desert. "*Nein, Herr* Major."

"Describe your location."

Richter peered into the darkness. "We're near a double oasis. I see several trees."

Lindisl translated to Abu. "Yes, I know the place, *effendi,*" Abu nodded. "They are far enough west. It is best if they turn southwest now. They will meet up with us soon."

Lindisl turned back to the radio. "Sergeant, change direction to southwest and catch up as soon as you can."

"*Jawohl, Herr* Major," Richter acknowledged.

Time passed. Abu leaned forward in his seat. "*Effendi,* they should be close now."

Lindisl commanded his driver, "Stop and turn off the engine." As they stood outside the vehicle, they heard a motor in the distance. Lindisl got back on the radio. "I hear you. I'll vector you in." In a few minutes, the halftrack pulled up beside the *kubelwagon.*

Richter jumped out and saluted, "Reporting as ordered, *Herr* Major."

As the two of them talked, Ali said something to Abu, who hurried over to Lindisl. "*Effendi*, if the American dogs are circling around to return to their comrades, there is a short cut we can take."

Lindisl whirled around. "Where is it?"

"Just a little further on, *effendi*."

"Would the Americans have taken it also?"

Abu shook his head. "Ali says unless they know about it, it is doubtful. The entrance is narrow and hard to notice."

"Can the halftrack go through?"

"It is narrow, it is doubtful."

Lindisl made his decision. "We will try it anyway, lead us to this shortcut." Abu bowed and conversed with Ali. The vehicles took off with the Arabs on their camels in the lead. Within a couple of miles, the Arabs turned off into a narrow defile. The halftrack made it through by scraping both sides. As they crept through the twisting defile, rising in altitude as they went, it widened the further they traveled. They reached the top and descended down the other side. Lindisl leaned forward in his seat, anticipating the victory almost in his grasp. When they debouched on the other side of the heights, Lindisl asked Abu, "How much distance did we save?"

"About thirty kilometers, *effendi.*"

"Good. We must be close behind them now."

They continued westward for about another hour. When red streaks heralded dawn they reached a height. One of the Arabs shouted and threw out his hand, pointing to the far side of a level area. They watched the dark blot of a vehicle coming close to a defile on the other side.

"I have them," Lindisl gloated. He called to check on the air support.

Chapter Thirty-Seven

Something caught Dane's attention in the mirror. He twisted the wheel and made the vehicle swerve so he could get a look behind them. Silhouetted against the morning light, he saw vehicles and riders on camels on a ridge top.

The sudden swerve roused Drew and Angelique. "What's wrong?" Drew asked, rubbing sleep out of his eyes.

"They're behind us."

"Who are behind us, Arabs or Germans?" The two of them twisted to look behind them.

"Both," Dane answered with a grim tone. They entered the defile and Dane glanced at the fuel gauge. It sat on empty.

"Are we going to make it, *mon chéri?*" Anxiety pitched Angelique's voice higher.

"I don't know, we're almost out of fuel. How much further do you think we have to go?" The last question Dane directed at Drew.

Drew bit his lip. "It can't be but a handful of miles now." The two men fell silent, trying to think of something, while Angelique stared white-faced at one and then the other.

Nearing the end of the defile, Dane grunted.

"I've got a plan. I'll stay here and block them as long as I can. You two take the halftrack and drive as far as it'll go. Then you'll have to walk. There are rifles in the back, use them for crutches."

"No," Drew shook his head. "You go and I'll stay. You can make better time than I can."

"With your leg, you have zero chance of escaping them. I do have the possibility. You have to take Angelique as far as you can in the vehicle. Who knows, the gauge might be off and you can make it to our lines."

"Or maybe not," Drew stated, staring at the other man.

"Or maybe not," Dane agreed.

Angelique stared at one and then the other. *Mon Dieu, I'll probably never see one of these men again. He'll sacrifice himself to save me and the other.* Her heart contracted with the pain of never seeing one of them again. But which one? Both of them were so dear to her heart. Which one could she not live without? Somehow she knew if she made the decision as to which one would stay and which one would go with her, they would acquiesce to her wishes. But she couldn't make the choice. She breathed a quick prayer, *Dear Jesus, if you will, save both of them.*

Dane braked to a stop, flung himself out of

the vehicle and ran around to the passenger door. He yanked the door open and pulled Drew out by his belt. Using his good arm, Dane hauled Drew over to the driver's door and shoved him inside. Dane grabbed his submachine gun and hollered, "Go, go," and started scrambling up the slope.

Drew slid beneath the wheel and took off. He turned an anguished face to Angelique. "Am I a coward for running away?"

Angelique reached out and patted his arm. "*Non,* you are not a coward, neither of you are. If anyone is a coward it is I. I could not make the decision which of you to go and which stays. It is as Dane said, he has the greater chance of surviving. I prayed for Jesus to spare you both."

Drew gripped the steering wheel, knuckles white from the force. "It's all we can do now, pray." They drove out of the defile, down another draw, up and over a ridge.

The engine started sputtering. It caught, went a little further, sputtered again, then died.

"Now we walk," Drew announced, trying to put on a cheerful face. With painful limbs they hobbled out of the cab and to the back of the halftrack. Drew pulled out two rifles which were within reach. Using them as crutches, they limped their way up a defile.

293

Behind them, Dane hid behind a boulder at the top of the slope where he watched for anyone coming down the defile. Sooner than he liked, he heard the sound of vehicles. First into sight were four Arabs riding camels, followed by a *kubelwagon*. Then, to Dane's dismay, a halftrack, filled no doubt with German soldiers. There were two camels tied to the back of the halftrack. He looked at his two hand grenades. He must make them count. He looked down onto the halftrack. A canvas cover protected those inside from the weather. He noticed a wide rent in it. If he could throw a grenade into the hole...He pulled the pins on both and flung them. The first hit in front of the *kubelwagon* and went off. The vehicle lurched sideways and stopped. On the halftrack, there were three braces holding up the canvas cover, with the canvas sagging down between them, the tear right in the middle of one of the sags. The second grenade lit on top of the canvas top in front of the hole, bounced over the hole and rolled up the slope of the canvas to almost where the brace held the canvas up, and then rolled back down and into the hole. It must have fallen amid gas cans, because when it blew up the whole halftrack burst into flames.

Dane opened fire with his submachine gun

upon the Arabs and saw them drop or fall to the ground. He nailed the driver as he bailed out of the burning halftrack. Dane missed the passenger as he sprang from the burning vehicle. Then Dane turned his attention to the *kubelwagon*. He sprayed it with bullets. His gun clicked empty. Frantic, he searched his person for spare ammo but found none. He checked his pistol, only two rounds were left. Stunned, he leaned back against the rock. If he just had one more clip of ammo, he could end this pursuit now. The enemy started firing back at him. There were at least two or three guns. He would have to leave. He slithered down the reverse side of the slope and took off after his friends.

Behind him, he left a shattered column. As the survivors laid down a covering fire, Ali slipped his way to where he could see behind the rock where the ambusher hid. He raised his gun and peeked out.

Empty.

At once he searched for other hiding spots, but found no trace of his archenemy. The Fox had escaped. He started cursing in anger and fear. How did this infidel keep ambushing and escaping from him?

Below in the defile, Major Lindisl shared the same feelings. The airfield told him the plane would be overhead in about half an hour. He tasted the sweet success of victory, when explosions suddenly ripped his troops apart. His *kubelwagon,* now a bullet riddled shambles, lay wrecked, the driver slumped over the wheel. The halftrack and the entire squad of soldiers except for the sergeant were gone, snuffed out in a second. Bullets penetrating Lindisl's vehicle from the top grazed his side. If he'd ducked the other way, he would be dead. Only Abu escaped injury. Of the Arabs, two more were dead. He could hear Ali yelling something and Abu shouted, "Stop shooting, the Fox has escaped."

They stopped firing and Lindisl turned questioning eyes towards Abu. "Escaped? He escaped?"

"The American infidel, he is a devil," and Abu shivered. Lindisl felt an answering quake.

Chapter Thirty-Eight

Dane took off jogging, following the tracks of the halftrack. He crossed another level place and entered a defile, slowing down to a walk. He followed them into a draw and scrambled up a ridge, his heart in his mouth. How far were they able to go? Did they have enough gas to reach the American line? At the top of the ridge he got his answer. He saw the abandoned vehicle a little ways ahead. He ran down the slope and up to the halftrack. He climbed into the bed and found another rifle, dropping his worthless submachine gun. He picked up as many spare clips of ammunition as he could and grabbed a canteen. Without giving the three cases of treasure another look, he dropped out and sped after his friends, following the holes in the ground made by the barrels of the guns they were using for crutches. He caught up to them in five minutes. His heart bled for them as he saw their limping progress.

"Oh *chéri*, you are alive," Angelique exclaimed, throwing her free arm around him while Drew pumped his arm with a huge grin on his face.

"We have to keep going, I couldn't stop all of them," Dane returned the hug while trying to explain his failure. "I ran out of ammo, I'm sorry." The tremor in his voice revealed his emotion at his lack of success.

Drew looked at Dane's contorted face in awe. *I can't think of another person who would try to stop such an enemy force singlehanded, and then apologize for not wiping it out.*

Dane handed Angelique's rifle to Drew. "Here, use both of the rifles, but don't try to fire them," he teased. Drew gave a grin back. He knew the barrels must be plugged by now. Dane wrapped an arm around Angelique and half-carrying, half-supporting her, took off at a much faster pace. Drew swung along using both rifles as crutches.

After about fifteen minutes, they came to a draw sloping upward and they stopped for a breather. A couple of minutes later they walked up the draw. When they reached the gap, the ground on both sides of them sloped upward another ten feet. On their right, level ground continued for about fifteen feet and then dropped in a steep decline, forming a shoulder. In front of them and to their left the terrain sloped down into a valley. On the other side of the valley they saw an encampment, with dark dots of people moving around and the shapes of stationary vehicles. Above them a flag snapped in the morning breeze, an American flag.

Drew raised both hands in the air, still gripping the rifles, "We did it, we did it, we made it."

Dane and Angelique each wrapped an arm around the other, and she heard him say under his breath, "Praise God, praise God. To Him all the glory."

A trickle of sand and gravel fell down the slope on their right. They looked up into four gun barrels pointing at them. Major Lindisl ordered, "Throw down your weapons."

When the three of them turned to look up the slope, Dane stood on the right, Angelique in the middle, and Drew, with his arms still raised in victory, on the left. They heard a sound, and Drew saw an Arab with a greying beard step around the shoulder and point his long rifle at them. Drew looked back up the slope; Major Lindisl stood in the middle holding a pistol. To his left, a German sergeant held a submachine gun on a sling, the gun tucked under his right arm pointing at them, the sling over his right shoulder. To Lindisl's right stood Abu and another Arab pointing long rifles at them.

Drew felt the bitter gall of defeat rising up in his throat, choking him. They were so close, SO CLOSE. How could they fail now? How could...

299

how could God let them down? He felt tears stinging his eyes as he lowered his arms. How did the enemy get there ahead of them? He'd heard no vehicle. The loud groan of a camel from behind the slope gave him his answer.

"Drop them, now," Lindisl ordered again. Drew watched as Dane threw his rifle to the ground in front of the sergeant, and then tossed his pistol and even his knife before raising his hands shoulder high.

Drew stood there irresolute, for one mad moment contemplating trying to shoot with the rifles in his hands. Maybe by some miracle they weren't clogged, maybe they would fire. He watched as all five weapons turned toward him. Reason won out and he dropped his rifles and pistol.

At the shoulder of the slope, Ali burned in his hate. Which one was the Fox? He'd used a submachine gun earlier, but neither of these two owned one. The tracks showed there were only the three of them left. He saw a taller, brown haired man and a shorter, dark haired man. From his angle, he didn't see the bandage on Drew's right leg. Ali watched the shorter man throw down his weapons and raise his hands in the air. The taller man stood there, and Ali read the emotions crossing the prisoner's face before he, too, threw down his weapons. He must be the Fox, Ali decided. He concentrated his gun and attention on him.

With the surrender of Drew, the four men at the top of the slope relaxed their guard. Lindisl and the sergeant started down the slope, followed by the Arabs, who, in order to keep their balance, lowered their guns.

"So we meet again," Lindisl gloated to Drew and Angelique. "We will have a very interesting conversation in a little while."

The sergeant reached Dane's guns and started to bend down to pick them up.

Everybody, Americans, Arabs, and Germans alike, were caught flatfooted with surprise when Dane exploded into action. With a snarling growl, he leaped the distance separating him from the sergeant. Dane yanked the knife out of the sheath which hung between his shoulders, the one he'd taken days before. He thrust the blade deep into the sergeant. Dane saw from the corner of his eye the Arab at the shoulder swing his rifle around. Dane twisted the sergeant's body between them, and felt the solid 'thunk' of the bullet hitting the dying German. At the same time, releasing the knife and holding the German upright with his right arm, Dane twisted the submachine gun with his left hand so the barrel pointed behind the German, and hung upside down. Dane pulled the trigger. The spray of bullets knocked down Lindisl and the two Arabs standing only feet away. Dane sent a fusillade into the Arab standing by himself. He fell backwards and didn't move. Then Dane saw Lindisl struggling to aim his pistol. Dane poured a hail of bullets into the German's chest. He flopped down, blood pouring from his wounds.

Like a primitive savage, Dane stood there among the dead and dying, with a snarl on his lips and green fire in his eyes.

Angelique screamed in white-faced terror at the sight of him. She turned and buried her face into Drew's shoulder.

Both men looked at her in astonishment and then at each other. They both realized in that instant, Angelique decided which man was for her.

Drew watched Dane release the German sergeant's body which slumped to the ground. Dane stood alone, the green vanishing from his eyes and naked pain on his face, listening to her sobs.

Chapter Thirty-Nine

None of them paid any attention to the sound of the airplane. Flight Sergeant Steutsel followed his revised morning schedule. Instead of taking off on another flight to the south, his planes were to be used to search for a German halftrack to the southwest. Sweeping out over the desert, his four planes soon lost sight of each other. As he scanned the ground, he spotted a stopped halftrack, with three camels next to it. He buzzed it and saw an Arab pulling cases out of the bed. "He's looting it, and no Germans in sight," he said to himself. He circled around again, and with guns blazing, cut down the Arab looter. He radioed, "Mission accomplished," and flew back to his base.

***

About three hours later, Angelique, Drew, and Dane faced each other at the American base. Patched up by the doctors, they were now saying their goodbyes.

Angelique clung to Drew's arm with a strained look on her face. She knew she'd broken Dane's heart. "*Chéri*, thank you for bringing Jesus to me, thank you for saving my life, thank you," she waved her free arm in her Gallic manner, "thank you for everything."

Dane's set face remained emotionless, but nothing could hide the pain in his eyes. At her words, he looked at her and his expression softened. "God bless," he said, his voice husky from suppressed feelings. "God bless you." He looked at Drew, "God bless both of you. I'm so glad both of you are saved." His throat chocked up and he couldn't go on.

Drew cleared his throat. "Yes, thank you for sharing Jesus with me too, and for saving my life, and everything else you've done. I have a few things to wrap up, and I'll need to see you in a few days. What is your outfit?"

"Second platoon, Company K, 26th Infantry," Dane answered.

Drew held out his hand, and felt relief when Dane took it. "I'll see you later, Dane."

Dane turned away, and as he walked away with his catlike walk, Angelique looked after him with an unfathomable look in her dark eyes. "He needs a wife who…," she paused, searching for the right words.

"Who can tame him?" Drew finished her sentence.

"*Non*," She shook her head with a vehement gesture. "*Non*, never tame." She kept the same unfathomable look in her eyes as she gazed at his disappearing figure. "He needs a wife who...can equal him. I could never be that woman. *Mon Dieu.*" Her eyes grew big as she added, "What a woman she would be." She turned and buried her head in Drew's shoulder again, much to the envy of those around them.

Six days later, Drew limped through a camp, looking for a certain person. He'd been told his quarry was here, and sure enough he found him. Although surrounded by men, somehow Dane seemed alone as he sat and cleaned his gun. Drew stopped and dropped a packet into his lap.

Dane looked up, and a smile crossed his lips. "Drew, I mean Captain Matthews." Dane scrambled to his feet and saluted.

Drew saluted back. "Drew is correct, and it's good to see you again, Dane."

Dane picked up the packet. "What's this?"

"Open it and find out."

Dane did, and found sergeant's stripes, a silver star, and a purple heart. He stared at them and then at Drew with a twisted smile. "So you get the girl and I get these."

"Don't knock it, Dane. It's entirely due to you we completed the mission and escaped." Drew pointed to the items. "This is the least I could do."

Dane gave a more natural smile. "Well, thank you for these."

"I hear your squad is being rebuilt."

"Yes, and then it's back to the front."

Dane held out his hand and Drew gripped it hard. "Thank you again for telling me about Jesus, for saving my life, and for making me a better officer."

"What?" Surprise washed across Dane's face. "What do you mean?"

Drew gave a wry smile. "I wasn't very good when you met me, but you taught me how to command."

"How did I do that?"

"By example."

Dane shook his head. "I didn't show you anything you didn't already have. What are your plans?"

"Angelique and I are going to Algiers and get married there. Then it's back to intelligence work for me." Drew waited a moment, "No warnings if I don't treat her right, you'll come back?"

"No," Dane grinned. "I know you'll be good to her, and besides," his grin became twisted, "she wouldn't want me anyway."

Battle of Kassarine Pass

When Hitler declared war on the United States in December, 1941. he and the German High Command knew it would take the Americans a year to put an army in the field. They also knew from historical fact it would take another year before the army would become battlefield proficient. The soldiers of every other country in the world needed to be in the war for a year before the soldiers learned how to fight and survive on the battlefield. The Americans landed an army in North Africa on November 8, 1942, eleven months and one day after Pearl Harbor.

When Rommel attacked the Americans at The Battle of Kassarine Pass, he found the Americans ill-positioned, low on supplies and their forces spread out. The green Americans, overwhelmed by superior forces and experienced generalship, routed for fifty miles. On the verge of a smashing victory which might turn the tide in Africa, at least for a while, Rommel ran out of support and supplies. Although urged on by his superiors, the wily Desert Fox knew he'd shot his bolt and retreated to his original positions.

The British used the poor showing of the

307

American troops for almost a year in degenerating American prowess. They did not understand Yankee ingenuity.

After the battle, the Americans removed many incompetent commanders and replaced them with able and aggressive men. The most notable exchange was the Second Corps commander General Fredendall being replaced by General Patton. The soldiers in the front lines learned much from their experience. When the American army fought again in just a few weeks, they gave a very different account of themselves. What it took the soldiers of Britain, Germany, Italy, China, Japan, Russia, France, and every other country in the world a year to learn, the American soldiers learned in one battle, The Battle of Kassarine Pass.

Utility Vehicles

Many of the armies in World War 2 possessed utility vehicles. They were used for a multitude of tasks, such as transporting wounded, supplies, light artillery and officers. Some of the more famous are the British Bren Carrier, over 50,000 produced, Russian GAZ-67 and the German *Kubelwagon,* also over 50,000 produced.

But the king of them all was the American Willys General Purpose ¼ ton 4x4 Utility Truck, shortened to GP and shortened further to jeep. It climbed steeper slopes, carried more weight and was more reliable than any other country's vehicles. American soldiers adapted them to any purpose they wanted. Over 600,000 were built, dwarfing the world's population of similar type vehicles. General Eisenhower regarded it as one of the five pieces of equipment most vital to the success in Africa and Europe. General Marshall called the vehicle "America's greatest contribution to modern warfare."

The jeep was another example of American industrial might and engineering ability which helped win the war.

Excerpt from Steadfast in Sicily

Book two of the Dane Shaw War Adventures

Almost an hour later Dane kneeled beside Lieutenant Jennings, the last conscious surviving officer. The lieutenant suffered multiple wounds but refused to be medicated, preferring to endure the pain and help organize the company. Dane gritted his teeth at the torn and suffering man and gave him a respectful salute. You're one of the good ninety day wonders. We can't afford to lose men like you.

"What's the story?" Jennings wheezed.

"I've got one of my men who understands German interrogating the prisoners, but we're not going to learn much more. We were been spotted by the Germans and a platoon ambushed us. It looks like they suffered about twenty casualties before breaking off."

The lieutenant gasped in pain. After catching his breath, he added, "I heard you caused seventeen of them."

At the obvious signs of acute pain, the medic standing by inserted a hyperemic needle into the patient's arm. As the morphine took effect, Dane watched the tortured lines in Jennings' face smooth out.

Dane shrugged at the complement and went on, "There're guards on each side of us and scouts are out looking for a place to take our wounded." He mopped his face with his shirt sleeve. "If we stay down here they'll cook. There has to be farmhouses or other buildings nearby. As for casualties, the company's been beheaded. Captain Carter, Lieutenants Galow and Wilson are dead and the medic says Lieutenant Oosterkamp probably won't survive his wounds. The First Sergeant and all four platoon sergeants are down, as well as seven other sergeants and five corporals. We have a total of 14 dead and 36 wounded, almost one third of the company."

***

Jennings looked at Sergeant Shaw through half closed eyes. The morphine shot the corpsman gave him started taking effect and his mind tried to drift away. He'd noticed when all the officers were down, Shaw issued orders which were effectual, economic, and brought organization out of the chaos.

Jennings' mind went back to the first exploding mortar shell. Either through incredible bad luck or very good aiming, it exploded right in the middle of the meeting called by Captain Carter.

The second landed close by. They devastated the command structure of the company. He could still hear the screams of the wounded and dying men and the pain as the shrapnel ripped into his own body.

He forced his mind back to the matter at hand. He'd been funneling orders through Shaw until now, but he wouldn't be able to hold up much longer. "Sergeant," he licked his dry lips, "you're gonna have to take command of the company, you're the senior surviving sergeant. I suggest we turn back." He sighed in resignation. He didn't like it, but he didn't know what else to do.

Dane pursed his lips. "Since we haven't seen any other American units, I expect the Germans have plugged the hole in their defenses and are between us and our lines. Has there been any radio contact with battalion?"

Jennings sighed. "We haven't been able to raise them, radio problems again." He paused. "They might have broken through and be following us."

Dane shook his head. "We can't rely on that. We have to assume we're on our own with a mission to accomplish. By the way, do you know where we are and where the bridge is?"

Jennings blinked in surprise. "Captain Carter

carried the map. Didn't you get it?"

Dane looked grim. "We didn't find it with his body, and I never saw it. So am I right to assume we don't know where we're going?"

Jennings grimaced again. "It looks like we can't go back, can't go forward, and can't stay here." He shot a look at the sergeant. "Maybe you should have a council of war with all the sergeants and see what they think."

"Sir," Dane hesitated and then with a dogged expression plowed on, "if I'm in command then I will command. I'm not going to stop and have a vote every time there needs to be a decision made. I'm open to ideas and suggestions, but I'll make the decisions."

Jennings looked at the determined face, satisfaction at Shaw passing his first test easing his mind. Jennings sagged. "Do you know what you're going to do?"

"Not yet, but God will show me," Dane replied, confidence in his voice.

Jennings drifted out again. What did Sergeant Shaw say, something about God? His mind retreated into a drug induced haze, blocking out the pain.

***

Corporal Winans came up, followed by

Private Braun, the German speaking man from Dane's squad. Like many people of German descent, Braun possessed brown hair and brown eyes. Winans saluted, "Lieutenant, burial detail is finished digging the graves." He stared at the lieutenant's white face and closed eyes.

Dane turned to him. "Lieutenant Jennings has turned the company over to me." He sighed. "I'll be there in a couple of minutes for the burials."

"Yes, Sarge," Winans hurried away.

Dane turned to Braun. "Did you get anything more out of the prisoners?"

Braun shook his head. "Just names, ranks, and serial numbers mostly."

"How about any other German units around, like their company?"

Braun hesitated. "I'm not sure; the company might be close by. Somebody said something before another prisoner hushed him up which might have meant they're an advance platoon for their company."

"Oh no," Dane moaned. "So we might be attacked by a company at any time." He looked around. "We have got to get out of here quick. Go join your squad for now; I'll need to detach you for guarding the prisoners later. Let Corporal Gates know."

314

After Braun left, Dane considered his next action. With the loss of all the officers he needed to appoint four new platoon leaders. He closed his eyes. Dear God, please give me wisdom. Direct me as to which four men I need to promote. In Jesus' name I pray. Amen.

He went over his mental notes of which sergeants kept their heads and which ones were overwhelmed by the disaster. Of course he knew all of them, kind of. His mind shied away like a nervous colt from the reason why he didn't know them better. Zimmerman was a lumberjack foreman from Minnesota. He keeps his men in line. Grissom is a heavy weapons sergeant. He needs to stay there. Lassiter's a tough Texan. He's a good fit. Jones is the senior surviving sergeant of his platoon and a good one. His choices made, he looked around and spotted one of them.

"Sergeant Zimmerman," he called out. He saw Zimmerman look up when he heard his name. Dane waited while Zimmerman finished giving instructions to Corporal Winans and then wasted no time in getting to the point. "Lieutenant Jennings has turned the company over to me. I'm putting you in charge of First Platoon, Sergeant Grissom over the Heavy Weapons Platoon, Sergeant Lassiter over the Second Platoon, and Sergeant Jones over the

Third. There might be a Kraut company nearby. If there is, the Germans who ambushed us have warned them. I need you to send a detail ahead and find a place where we can take the wounded out of this riverbed and defend ourselves from an attack."

Zimmerman nodded. "I'll send out a squad right away. Anything else?"

Dane added, "I want to hold a conference with the four of you. I'll need to round the others up. Do you know where they are?"

Zimmerman looked at him. "Um, you could send runners to find them."

Dane looked at him with a blank stare and then shook his head in self-disgust. "You're right, I didn't think about them." He looked around. "Do you know where they are?"

Zimmerman chuckled. "I'll send them out. Where and when do you want to meet?"

Dane glanced up and pointed to a big rock at the top of the slope. "Meet there in ten minutes," he looked at his watch, "at 1045 hours. I need some fresh air. Now I have to hold the funeral."

Dane moved off and pulled his well-read Bible out of his pocket. When he got to the grave site, some of the men were standing around. He started reading from Psalms 104, starting at verse 13: "Like as a father pitieth his children, so the Lord pitieth them that fear him. For He knoweth our frame; he remembereth that we are dust."

* * *

When Braun climbed the slope to return to his squad, he met Conners standing watch.

"Did you learn anything from your cousins?" Conners asked, his ever-present cigarette drooping from the corner of his mouth.

Always sensitive about his German heritage, Braun swore and turned on him. "Don't call me a Kraut!" he yelled and swung a punch, catching the surprised Conners in the face, giving him a bloody lip and smashing his cigarette. The two men started punching each other. Braun dropped his rifle and swung a right at Conners' head. Conners ducked, the blow missed, and then hit Braun in the face, snapping his head back.

In a rage, Braun rushed Conners, smothering him with a succession of rights and lefts. Conners put up a desperate defense, trying to block the blows with his forearms as he gave up ground. Then his heel caught on a rock and he tripped and fell down with Braun on top of him. Braun felt hands grabbing and pulling him off before he could land another blow. Rosario held him while O'Halloran yanked Conners to his feet.

Gates came storming up, yelling "What's

317

going on here?", or words to that effect.

"He called me a Kraut," Braun accused.

"I just asked if he learned anything from the prisoners," Conners whined. "I didn't call him a Kraut."

Gates looked at both of them in disgust. "If you want to fight somebody, there's a whole German-Italian army out there. Go fight them. Braun, stop being so thin-skinned. Conners, get back to your post." Rosario and O'Halloran released their grips and Conners wiped his mouth. When he saw the blood on it, he glared at Braun and slouched away, pulling out another cigarette.

Braun mopped his sweaty face and looked at Gates while the other two went back to their posts. "Sergeant Shaw wanted me to tell you he's going to dispatch me to guard duty over the prisoners."

"Did he say when?"

"No." Braun shook his head, and then added, "What a mess. We got whipped, a sergeant's in command of the company, and I don't think he knows what to do."

Gates gave him a cold stare. "You've only been with the squad a couple of weeks. You'll soon find out Sergeant Shaw always has a plan. As for being whipped, you're only beaten if you think so. Now get back to your post."

***

Although Dane didn't hear what Braun said, he saw the words echoed in his men as he moved among them. The body language and the side-long looks let him know the men were dispirited by the defeat and disquieted at being led by a sergeant. A sergeant many of them knew little about. Since becoming promoted to sergeant, he'd held himself apart from most of the men for personal reasons. As a result they didn't know him. Expressions told him some of the men were whipped, but a disgusted comment he overheard summed up the attitude of many others: "Ambushed by a platoon. A platoon, for crying out loud!"

When he gave orders to prepare the wounded to be carried up the slope, he noticed just the hope of them getting out of the oven of the riverbed made the men perk up. Many of them weren't beaten yet, but if he didn't come up with something soon, they well might be. If only I knew what to do?

He noticed the group of sergeants standing at the meeting place. He climbed up to give them their new assignments.

While Dane talked to the new platoon leaders, Tennessee and Hemphill were out scouting for someplace to take the wounded: a farmhouse, an empty barn, something. They were about half a mile away from the company and hadn't seen anything yet. They were climbing a rocky ridge when they heard movement on the other side. They froze, listening. Tennessee motioned for Hemphill to cover him. He crawled up and peered around a rock, to see a face staring back at him from a few inches away.

www.ingramcontent.com/pod-product-compliance
Lightning Source LLC
Chambersburg PA
CBHW060400260626
47160CB00006B/2381